Forevermore

CINDY MILES

Point

*For Deidre Knight, Aimee Friedman,
and Becky Shapiro. You are Magic
Dream Makers.*

No part of this publication may be reproduced, stored in a retrieval system, or
transmitted in any form or by any means, electronic, mechanical, photocopying,
recording, or otherwise, without written permission of the publisher. For
information regarding permission, write to Scholastic Inc., Attention:
Permissions Department, 557 Broadway, New York, NY 10012.

Library of Congress Cataloging-in-Publication Data

Miles, Cindy.
Forevermore / by Cindy Miles. — 1st ed.
p. cm.
Summary: When sixteen-year-old Ivy starts a new life in her stepfather's castle
in Scotland, she finds that her stepfather's grandmother is implacably hostile
and some mysterious spirit in the castle is trying to injure her — and her new
best friend is a ghost named Logan.
ISBN 978-0-545-42622-0
1. Magic — Juvenile fiction. 2. Castles — Scotland — Juvenile fiction. 3. Ghost
stories. 4. Stepfamilies — Scotland — Juvenile fiction. 5. Scotland — Juvenile
fiction. [1. Magic — Fiction. 2. Castles — Fiction. 3. Ghosts — Fiction.
4. Stepfamilies — Fiction. 5. Family life — Scotland — Fiction. 6. Scotland —
Fiction.] I. Title.
PZ7.M594313For 2013
813.6 — dc23
2012035275

12 11 10 9 8 7 6 5 4 3 2 1   13 14 15 16 17/0

Printed in the U.S.A.   40
First edition, July 2013
Book design by Yaffa Jaskoll

Thig crioch air an t-saoghal, ach mairidh gaol is ceòl.

The world will end but love and music endure.

SCOTTISH GAELIC PROVERB

Chapter 1

The faint outline of my face reflects off the glass as I stare out the window of my stepdad's pewter Jaguar. The cold outside seems to reach clear to my bones. My breath fogs the glass, and I wipe it with a finger and continue to watch the scenery flash by.

Stark, jagged cliffs of gray rock. Desolate moors. White signs written first in Gaelic, then English. Old stone houses, whitewashed, pop up every once in a while. The sky is dramatic, with enormous swirling dark clouds. Everything actually looks cold. Or dead. Maybe that's because I'm from Charleston, South Carolina, and I'm used to the sultry weather there. I already miss it, too. The constant warm sea breeze, the palm trees and ancient oaks draped in moss, the old plantations. Funny how I took all that for granted when I lived there. Now that I don't have it anymore, I want it back.

Like I still want my dad back. He died the week after my thirteenth birthday and it's been just me and Mom for the past three years. Until now.

"Oh, honey! Look at the sheep," my mom says excitedly, and points out the window. "Look at their little black faces. They are so adorable!"

I don't answer, because *honey* is an endearment reserved for my stepdad, Niall. He chuckles and lightly grazes Mom's cheek with his knuckle. I bet he doesn't find the sheep nearly as adorable as my mom does. Neither turns to ask my opinion.

I glance over anyway and, sure enough, there are the adorable black-faced sheep, standing in a white downy cluster on the side of a hill dotted with purple-brown heather. I'd Googled heather before we got here, and saw that in June and July, the lifeless clumps would turn into gorgeous lavender blooms. But now, in October, those blooms are so dead.

Pulling my legs up, I lean my head against the window and close my eyes. So much has happened lately, it's strange to think of it all in sequence. It's even stranger to think this is my life now. Before my dad died, I was your typical kid — except for being freakishly excellent at playing the violin. I hung out with my friends, had sleepovers, watched hours of classic scream fests, like the old *Halloween* and *Nightmare on Elm Street* movies. And since we lived only two blocks from the beach, my friends and I gathered there nearly every weekend. I had a big poster of Zac Efron from his *High School Musical* days hanging on the ceiling above my bed, so I could stare at him as I went to sleep.

But after my dad died? I don't know. Things just didn't seem to have the same appeal to me anymore. I withdrew. Where I had been loud and silly and voracious before, I became quiet, and I wanted to be alone more often. My circle of friends grew smaller and smaller as I became more reclusive. Callie, my best friend, hung on the longest. But even she began to distance herself, growing closer to other girls. By the time I left for Scotland, it just . . . wasn't a huge deal that I was leaving. We hugged, said good-bye, and promised to keep in touch. Maybe to even see each other over long breaks. I doubt it'll happen, though. And honestly? It's okay. I became a major downer for a long time, and didn't expect my friends to be dragged down with me.

Hopefully this move will make things better. Maybe I'll meet some cool people at school, make new friends who will like and accept me for who I am now.

I rest my cheek against the cool glass, scroll my iPod to another playlist. I'm feeling a little old-school today, so Madonna's "Material Girl" plays through the earbuds as I continue to stare out at the wispy ribbons of mist.

I still enjoy many things that my dad and I shared, especially books, movies, and music. Dad started me on reading old mysteries, like Nancy Drew and Sherlock Holmes, which I still love. And because of Dad, I am one serious '80s music fangirl. Dad always said I was an '80s girl trapped in a twenty-first-century body. AC/DC, Whitesnake, Cyndi Lauper, Madonna — you name it. It definitely inspires the violin music that I compose and play.

Which brings me to the most important thing that my dad introduced me to: the violin. I've been playing since I was three years old. My dad gave me my first instrument — a miniature working violin that he found at a yard sale, of all places. I still have it, too. It almost looks like a toy, but it really plays. And as young as I was,

I totally remember my dad putting that violin in my hands, adjusting my fingers over the neck, and squeezing my other little hand over the bow. I don't know why I didn't do what other normal three-year-olds would've done with a violin — which is whack something with it — but I just . . . played. And I haven't stopped since. It's a part of me. And when my dad died, my mom picked right up with the support of my music. She makes sure I never slack on my strings.

I shift in the seat and tug the sleeves of my oversized sweater down over my hands. A light rain has started to fall from the charcoal sky. It seems even darker than before.

In the driver's seat, Niall announces, not so much to me, but aloud, that we are *verra* close. That's how the word *very* sounds when he speaks it and it's one of just a handful of his words I can now understand.

Two months ago, my mother married Niall MacAllister, a Scottish laird. A laird is equal to something sort of like a a duke. He's rich and lives in a castle in the Scottish Highlands. That's where we're headed now. To a freaking castle. I still can't believe I've left my home in Charleston and crossed the Atlantic to come here.

Niall is good-looking, for an older guy: tall, with sandy hair and blue eyes. And I can see how some might find his Scottish accent charming. But he and I haven't exactly clicked yet. With me, he's short, abrupt, and not very conversational. He has no kids himself, so maybe he just doesn't get teenagers. Mom picks up on the chill between me and Niall, but she doesn't know what to do about it.

I know my mom deserves to be happy, though. She's worked as an ER nurse for as long as I can remember, and raised me by herself after Dad died. She did a pretty good job, being a single mom. But Mom and Niall have only known each other for less than a year. He could be a real jerk, or a serial killer or something. I guess we'll soon find out.

Mom and Niall say that it must have been fate that led him to Mom's emergency room. He was in Charleston on real-estate business, and had nearly sliced off his thumb with a tire iron while changing a flat. Mom's beautiful, with thick, wavy blonde hair and a bubbly personality. She told me Niall couldn't keep his eyes off her the entire time the ER doc sewed his thumb up. Sometimes I'm surprised it took my mom as long as it did to find someone else. But Dad was a pretty hard act to follow.

Everyone says I look just like my dad, with fair skin and gray-blue eyes. My long blonde hair is as straight as hay, but recently I had a pink streak put in and I love it. It reflects my violin music, which is part punk, part Victorian. I like to think I'm part punk, part Victorian myself. Part Victorian because, despite my standoffish manner, I'm truly a romantic. No one, except maybe my old friend Callie, really knows that side of me. I prefer to keep it that way, too.

We're passing a sign that says "Glenmorrag," and Niall points down a side road.

"That track there will take you straight to the village," he says in his thick accent. He glances at me in the rear-view mirror. "Smaller than what you're accustomed to, I suppose, but you'll get used to it. There's a grocer, a library, a baker and butcher, and the fishmonger. And a petrol station. We've one chip shop, one restaurant and pub, and one inn. The high school is in the next village."

I tense up. Today is Friday. I'll be starting at that high school come Monday.

Niall turns his head to Mom and smiles at her. "A chip shop is where they sell fresh fried fish-and-chips. 'Tis the best in the Highlands. You'll love it, Lady MacAllister."

It's crazy to think Mom is officially a "Lady" now. What does that make me? I'm not sure. I shake my head and stare down the path, but all I see are tall, thick pines half swallowed up by the mist. I shiver. Are there wolves running through the forests?

"It looks pretty dark in there," Mom says.

"Aye," Niall agrees. "But once you get closer to the village, it opens up to the sea."

Mom turns around to peer at me. Her eyes are wide. "Isn't this exciting, Ivy? We'll have to go into the village together soon, okay?" She wiggles her brows. "They have a library, did you hear?"

I smile at that. It's hard not to smile at my mom's enthusiasm. "We can get membership cards, huh, Mom?"

"Absolutely." She grins and turns back around.

Now we're on a narrow gravel road lined with thick brush and tall pines. We start a slow climb, the Jag's tires crunching against rocks. The mist has grown so heavy that visibility can't be more than a few feet in some places. It's like looking through chowder.

"Hold on, love," Niall says to Mom. He laces his fingers through hers. "Almost there."

The Jag peaks and levels as we reach the top of the

hill. Looming ahead is something straight out of the pages of Bram Stoker or Edgar Allan Poe. Mom gasps. I nearly do, too.

A massive medieval fortress made of gray-and-black stone stretches before us and hugs the edge of the craggy sea cliffs. Four imposing towers, one on each corner, rise above the estate grounds. We come to a stop in front of the heavy black wrought-iron gates, and my heart begins to pound. I'm going to *live* here? It isn't a stuffy, manicured castle. Instead it's . . . menacing. Barely a notch above ruinous. And it completely fascinates me.

Niall presses a button and the gates swing open with an ear-piercing creak and groan of metal against metal. As Niall drives through, I turn in my seat and watch those iron gates slowly close, locking us inside. An unfamiliar feeling of dread grips me.

A flock of ravens rises like a black cloud out of an ancient-looking tree. Most of the orange, red, and yellow leaves have already fallen off the trees and they lay scattered about on the ground. I think about the fact that Halloween is in a couple of weeks.

As soon as Niall puts the Jag in park, I grab my violin case and shoulder it, open the door, and slide out. It's stopped raining. The icy wind stings my cheeks, and I pull my red knit hat farther down to cover my ears. Mist slips through the air in front of my face, and I drag my hand through it and watch it swish around my fingers. The mist is almost alive, the way it's constantly shifting, drifting.

The air smells clean and sweet, a mixture of something that reminds me of clover with the salty tang of the sea — an odd and striking contrast to the gloomy doom of the estate. Other than the crackle of dead leaves, the rubbing of dead branches, and the occasional caw of a raven, it's eerily still. If I strain my ears, I can hear the sea bashing against the base of the rocky cliffs.

"Spooky, aye?" Niall says to Mom, and the two stand in front of me while they take in the view. My stepfather is ridiculously tall, especially compared to Mom's short five feet three inches. And I'm an inch shorter than her. Niall points toward the top of the castle. "Up there's our fierce gargoyle watchmen. You can barely see them through this blasted mist. Quite frightening up close, and there's a different one on every eave." A lighthearted chuckle escapes his throat. It makes me wish he could be more like this all the time. "I loved playing here as a wee lad. Loads of fantastic hiding places all over the estate."

I shudder. The gargoyles do look freaky — like creepy, distorted little stone men, crouched and watching. Waiting to fling themselves down at you and grab you.

"Oh, Niall, it's amazing!" Mom cries, and throws her arms around him.

Niall hugs my mom fiercely. "I'm happy you're here with me. My verra own family." He gives me a quick, uncomfortable glance. "You too, Ivy." I bite my lip and stick my hands in my pockets. Niall tries to break the awkward moment. "Right," he says, the *r* rolling from his tongue. "You two should go in and get settled. I want to introduce you to my grandmother and the staff."

With a heavy sigh, I brace myself. New people. New home. Totally different country. A little overwhelming to say the least.

Before we make it to the enormous wooden doors, they open. A petite elderly lady comes forward, followed by a man and woman in servant uniforms, who head to the car to get our luggage. But it's the old woman who demands attention. Even at twenty feet away, I can tell she's not one to mess with. With her nose tilted upward, her sharp chin jutting out, and her white-gray hair pulled into a tight bun, she carries an air about her that is unmistakable. Wealth. Snotty wealth. And boy, she wears it proudly. I'm instantly annoyed.

"Grandmother!" shouts Niall, and hurries forward to embrace her. "I've a verra special girl for you to meet," he tells her.

The old lady's gaze lands straight on me. Her mouth draws tight and her eyes narrow. She glances from the case I have slung over my shoulder to my Converse All Stars to the holes in my jeans, the pink streak in my hair, and then back at my face as though smelling something putrid. I hold my ground, set my jaw, and stare right back. A weighty silence suspends between us.

"Julia," says Niall, draping an arm over Mom's shoulders, "this is my grandmother, Lady Elizabeth. Grandmother, my wife, Lady Julia MacAllister." He clears his throat. "And this is her daughter, Ivy."

Which, to me, translates to "And this is her baggage, Ivy."

Elizabeth's gaze grows even colder, and then slowly slips over to Mom, who gives a polite nod.

"It's so nice to meet you, Elizabeth," Mom says in her sweet Charleston drawl. "Niall speaks so highly of you." Class. My mom definitely has class.

A forced smile stretches across Elizabeth's mouth. "My grandson has spoken quite highly of you as well." Her accent is more clipped, more polished than Niall's. She glances at me. The fake smile disappears, replaced by another pinched look. "Come. Supper awaits us."

With that, she turns on her little black heels and glides through the double doors.

Niall tugs my mom's hair playfully. "Och, dunna let old Granny worry you," he says. I've learned that *dunna* is his way of saying *don't*. "She doesna take well to strangers. She just likes to make sure everyone knows she's the boss of Glenmorrag."

Mom smiles. "She's fine, Niall. She's related to you, after all. It won't take her long to warm up."

I don't believe Grandmother Elizabeth will warm up one little bit.

Just then, a piercing screech cracks the air. I feel a jolt of fear as I peer through the fog for the source of the noise. An unsettled feeling creeps over my skin.

When the noise comes again, I'm sure it's a woman's scream.

Chapter 2

◦⧽ GLENMORRAG ◦⧽

*M*om stifles her own scream as Niall chuckles and puts a hand on her shoulder. "Dunna worry, darlin'. 'Tis nothing more than those crazy-eyed peacocks," he says, pointing. "See there? They love nothing better than to roost in the trees."

I follow Niall's gaze, and find several blue-bodied peacocks settled into their roosts, high in an aged oak. One stretches its neck and cries out. I swear, it sounds *exactly* like a woman's scream. My teeth chatter, and I rub my arms through my heavy sweater.

"Let's go inside," says Niall. He and Mom turn and I follow, glancing up at the castle's imposing facade. A slight movement catches my eye in a small window close to the top of the castle wall. It's high enough up that I can't tell if someone is standing there. I squint, trying to see through the fading light and thick mist. But I see nothing.

I *feel* something, though. As if eyes are on me, watching my every move.

The feeling doesn't go away once I'm inside the castle. Is someone behind me? I freeze, still as death, and glance over my shoulder. Nothing. Slowly, I exhale. I'm probably just letting my imagination run crazy.

Stone walls and black wooden rafters make up the enormous great hall. There are three circular chandeliers made of old deer antlers, and a fireplace large enough to walk into. Brass sconces light the hall with a blushed amber glow. At the far end is a large staircase, with one of those menacing gargoyles perched on top of the bannister. There are some other curiosities I'll have to explore later, things I'll want to see up close, like the tall, dusty suit of armor in the corner.

Very different from the small two-bedroom carriage-house apartment Mom and I shared in Charleston. I glance around and swallow a lump of apprehension.

Like it or not, this is home sweet home.

Niall turns to me. "Ivy, your chamber is on the third

floor, last door on the right. You've the place to yourself up there, and it's equipped with Wi-Fi." He tells Mom, "Our chamber is on the second floor, love. Grandmother's is on the first."

At least I'm far from *her*.

Mom beams at me. "Isn't this great, Ivy? I already love it, don't you?"

I give Mom a smile, although it feels about as fake as Elizabeth's looked. "Sure, Mom," I say. I don't tell her that my stomach is full of rabid butterflies. Or that I wish Niall would at least show me to my room. I guess he figures I'm mature and can handle it myself. And I can. I will.

Mom waves. "I'll see you in a bit." Then Niall whisks her off to show her the kitchen and introduce her to the staff.

I sigh, sling my violin case higher, and start up the stairs. On my way, I get a good look at the ghoulish gargoyle. Its face, fanged and misshapen, stares right at me.

The higher I climb, the darker and colder it becomes, and by the time I reach the third floor, only the scant yellowish light from the wall sconces shines a path across the hardwood hall. A faded rug stretches the length of the corridor. Against the wall halfway to my room sits a lone straight-backed wooden chair. The silence unnerves me.

At the last door on the right, I stop, turn the brass handle, and throw open the heavy oak.

My new room.

I walk in and gape at a space that's easily as large as our old apartment. My bags have already been brought up and placed neatly against the wall. A mahogany armoire stands in the far corner, and a small writing desk and lamp sit beside the bed. At the foot of the bed is a medieval-looking wooden chest, covered in etchings and bands of iron.

I walk over to the massive bed. The mattress comes up to my waist, and the four mahogany posts nearly reach the ceiling. A gray plaid curtain made of wool hangs on a wooden rod that circles the bed. I can close myself in when I sleep if I want.

I guess it's nice to have the privacy, alone on the third floor. But then my imagination runs wild again. Someone could slip in at any time and kidnap me. Murder me in my sleep. And no one would even hear me if I screamed. . . .

I try to shake off these thoughts. I walk over to the big picture window beside the fireplace. The same scratchy-looking gray plaid wool not only covers the window seat but is also used for drapes. I push the curtains aside and peer out.

The shadowy cliffs completely drop off into the sea, eerily beautiful. An entire panorama of the west side of Glenmorrag's grounds can be seen. At the farthest corner, I make out what looks to be a stone ruin, right on the property. Intriguing.

"'Tis the old rectory. A fine, cavernous grotto to explore," a clipped, proper voice says, making me jump.

I spin around to see an old man in a pressed gray suit standing in my doorway. He was one of the servants who took our luggage from the car.

"'Twas built in 1789," he continues, nodding out the window toward the ruin. He must notice I still looked startled by his presence, because one corner of his mouth lifts, and he gives a short bow. "I am Jonas, young lady, and I am Glenmorrag's steward. Let me know if I can be of any assistance at all. Supper will be served in fifteen minutes. And the toilet — err, the bathroom, as you Yanks call it — is just across the hall. There's a pantry within. It should contain all necessities."

"Thanks, Jonas," I say, relaxing. He seems friendly. Almost grandfatherly.

He winks, and flicks something from his sleeve. "Lady Elizabeth doesn't fancy waiting. She gets a bit cross when her tummy rumbles."

I nod. "I can imagine that." I seriously doubt a rumbling tummy is the only thing that makes Elizabeth cross.

Jonas gives the vaguest of grins, then turns and disappears out the door. I decide I like him. He has a twinkle in his eye that screams rebel to me.

I quickly freshen up in the bathroom, then make my way back down the dim corridor and downstairs for supper.

I'm not sure what I was expecting to find in the dining room, but it wasn't a long, formal table set with silver and fine china. Niall and Mom are already seated, and Mom gives me a comforting smile. Grandmother MacAllister watches me closely.

"You can take your place there," she says, inclining her head to a setting.

"Thanks." I tuck my hair behind my ear and glance around. Four servers are standing behind the table in a line, waiting. For me, I suppose. I can't believe there is so much fuss over four people eating dinner.

Once I'm seated, the food is served: first a course of bland pea soup, followed by beef tips, seasoned potatoes, and sautéed vegetables. It's fine, but I want nothing more than to sit with Mom in our tiny kitchen in Charleston and eat a burger and fries. All this formal stuff is too much.

I peer at Elizabeth over the rim of my glass. Her skin is so thin and pale, blue veins peek out from the white face powder she's applied liberally. She has on a dress and heels. On her index finger I notice an elaborate ruby ring in a square setting, set in gold. It's the deepest red I've ever seen.

I have on the same outfit I traveled in: big sweater, skinny jeans with holes in the knees, sneakers. I can't help but wonder if Elizabeth will eventually insist I dress for dinner. I hope not.

"Is your room sufficient, Ivy?" Niall asks.

I nod, surprised Niall's even speaking to me. "Big," I say after I've finished chewing a mouthful of potatoes.

"Aye," he answers. A moment later he adds, "There's an enormous maze out back, in the gardens, that you might like."

I'm not sure what to say, so I nod. "Cool."

Elizabeth meticulously sets her fork and knife aside,

wipes her mouth with the cloth napkin, and turns toward me. I steel myself.

"There are rules here, young lady," Elizabeth begins. "Rules which you will be expected to obey." Her frosty gaze locks onto me. "For one, holes in your clothes at the family table are unacceptable."

Knew it. I shoot a glance at Mom, who looks troubled by this statement.

"And it's more than clear that you need quite a bit of etiquette training," Elizabeth adds. Her eyes harden. "Sit up straight."

I don't move. The entire room goes silent as a graveyard. I don't even know how to respond.

"Gran," Niall says to Elizabeth, surprising me again. "'Tis no way to start out with Ivy here. Times have changed, you know," he coaxes. "Ivy's fine. Now," he says, changing the subject, "tell my new bride here of your first days at the castle, aye?"

I look gratefully at Niall, and my mom eases a pleading gaze my way.

I know Mom. She doesn't like how Elizabeth just spoke to me, but she doesn't want to make enemies with her, either.

Niall's question seems to do the trick. The MacAllister matriarch turns her attention to Mom and Niall. I stifle a sigh of relief.

A genuine smile touches Elizabeth's lips. "'Twas the grandest day of my life, the day I first set foot in Glenmorrag," she says. "The village, with its cobblestones and stone walls and little shops. And this place." She glances around. "I . . . couldn't believe it was mine. The castle needed a woman's touch, that was for certain. I replaced the tartan fabrics, hired some help, and had it cleaned from top to bottom. At the same time, your grandfather's distilleries began to do exceedingly well. That's when I . . ."

Her voice trails off. And her eyes harden.

"Aye, Grandmother?" Niall urges.

"Nothing. 'Twas a long time ago." Elizabeth then picks up her fork and knife, and begins to eat, ignoring us all. Niall looks at Mom and gives a slight shrug. Weird. Could she be senile? I wonder. She *is* really old.

By this time I've eaten my fill, so, in my most polite voice, I excuse myself to head back upstairs. I can only take so much of Elizabeth. Mom seems to understand — she blows me a kiss and wishes me good night.

The scream of the wind pushes at the cracks of the castle walls as I hurry to my new room. Once inside, with the door closed, I breathe easier. I decide to unpack before bed. Maybe I'll feel more settled then.

As I open the armoire, I think about starting at my new school on Monday. I wonder how it's going to be. I've gone to school with the same group of kids most of my life. Now I'll be joining a class in the middle of their semester, or whatever it's called here. Everyone already has friends. I'm American, so that will probably make me a point of interest. Who knows? I do know I have to wear a uniform, which really bites.

I'm folding my last sweater when the hairs on the back of my neck turn stiff. Suddenly, I hear the moan of a bow being dragged across the strings of a violin. I whip around.

My violin is suspended in midair. I feel my knees go weak and I try to scream but nothing comes out.

My violin is being played in midair by . . . no one.

I blink. Just that fast, the instrument flies and lands on the bed. I let out a small shriek and rush over to it. I grab the violin and bow and hug them to my chest as I frantically scan the room.

The weighty presence of *something* lingers, but the room is empty. I even drop to my knees and peek underneath the bed.

Nothing is there. No one. Not even a dust bunny.

But I know what I saw. I jump up and head for the door. I have to tell Mom what just happened. As I fling open the door, though, I find Jonas standing there.

"Miss Ivy, is there something the matter?" he asks. "I heard a scream."

"I —" I begin, and glance behind me, then back toward Jonas. "I . . . s-saw something weird," I finally stammer.

A look of understanding crosses Jonas's face but it's quickly replaced by one of concern. "What was it?" he asks. He peers over my shoulder into my room.

I stare at him, unsure of what to say. If I tell him what I saw, I'll sound like a lunatic. If I tell *Mom* what I saw, I will as well. She'll think I'm acting out, trying to find an excuse to go home.

"Are you sure you're not just overly tired, miss?" Jonas asks. "Jet lag can do strange things to a person." He gives me a reassuring smile. "I'll fix you a nice cup of hot tea and bring it straightaway. Tea fixes everything, you know."

I smile back, feeling my heart rate slow down a bit. "Sure, that sounds great." Maybe he's right. Maybe I am just jet-lagged.

As I wait for Jonas to return with the tea, I hover by the door, still a little afraid to go back fully inside the room. But my violin and bow lay innocently on my bed, and the eerie feeling that was here earlier seems to have lifted.

Suddenly, I feel a deep sense of emptiness. It's not like me to wallow in self-pity. But this new situation is making me realize how utterly alone I am. Mom and Niall are wrapped up in each other. My dad is gone. I have no siblings, grandparents, or even aunts and uncles that I'm close to. My step-grandmother has apparently decided to hate my guts. My friends back home — if I can even call them friends anymore — are an ocean away. I fight the urge to cry. Jonas will be back soon and he doesn't need to see me sniffling and sobbing.

Within a few moments, he returns with a tray, and on it a pot of steaming-hot tea, a flowery cup and saucer, sugar cubes, cream, and a tiny little spoon. Three thick, rectangular cookies sit upon a frilly napkin. "Here you are, young lady," he says, placing the tray on my bedside table. "Tea, and some shortbread to go with it. If you should need anything else, my chambers are behind the kitchen downstairs."

"Thank you," I say, realizing Jonas is the closest thing I have to a friend right now. "I really appreciate it."

"My pleasure," he responds, then quietly leaves me alone.

As I sip the tea and chomp on the cookies — shortbread, I remind myself — I do start to feel better. I even get brave enough to walk over to my violin and bow and lift them up, feeling their familiar weight. *It was just your imagination*, I tell myself.

I take my violin to the window and find a comfortable spot on the window seat. Outside, the Highlands are covered in inky darkness. With a sigh, I drag my bow over the strings and begin to play, improvising. The melody that comes out is soft, yet powerful. The melancholy sound fits my mood as I gaze out into the shadows of the moors.

Chapter 3

∽ THE HAUNTING ∽

My eyes pop open. I bolt up in bed, confused.

Remembering.

What had happened in the middle of the night? Was it real? I think back.

I'd lain awake in the huge bed for hours, trying to fall asleep. It seemed as though everything hit me at once — memories of Dad, memories of getting suspended from school for cutting class to play violin at a festival two counties over, memories of Callie and other friends — you name it, I thought about it. I'd also listened to every creak and groan coming through the walls of the castle.

Then, just as my eyes had finally drifted shut, I'd heard it. At least, I think I heard it. So soft, I'd nearly missed it. Could I have even dreamed it? I'm pretty sure I didn't.

"Begone! Leave here at once!"

My eyes had flashed open. It was a deep, scratchy voice — a guy's voice — with a thick Scottish accent. The words were so clear it was as if someone had spoken them right into my ear. But how could that be? I got up, turned on the lights, and searched the room, not sure of what I was expecting, but certain something unnatural lurked close by. I never found anything, but the feeling never went away, either.

Finally, I'd fallen asleep.

And now it's morning. Though it's not as bright and airy as my home in Charleston was, the castle feels much less gloomy in the light of day. Slipping from the bed, I pull on a pair of jeans, my All Stars, and a thick pumpkin-colored sweater. I also drape my coat over my arm, stuffing my knit hat into the pocket. Maybe I'll take a walk after breakfast.

When I get downstairs, I run right into Elizabeth coming out of her room.

"You're late," she says, and her jaw tightens. "I will not tolerate *late*."

I stare at her, speechless. "For — for breakfast? I . . . didn't know there was a specific time —"

"There's always a specific time," Elizabeth interrupts. Although she's petite, in her black heels, we are eye to eye.

So quickly I almost miss it, Elizabeth's cold eyes change. In color? Or size? Something undefined about them shifts.

Whatever it is, it's . . . frightening.

"And you'd best not be late again." Elizabeth lowers her voice. "Or *else*."

I recoil, mostly out of shock that she's being so harsh. The corner of her mouth lifts in a grin that reminds me of one of the gargoyles', and she turns and struts to the dining room.

Did Elizabeth MacAllister, who might be close to a hundred, just threaten me?

"Lost, miss?"

I jump at this new voice. A young maid stands near me, looking at me with wide, questioning eyes.

"Ah, no," I respond. "Just headed to the dining room. Thanks, though."

The maid gives a nod, and I cross the great hall. When I push through the swinging oak doors, everyone is seated. Waiting.

Great. I slip into my seat. As we eat, Niall and Mom discuss their plans for their day — taking care of things around the house — and Elizabeth is silent. Stone-faced. I make short work of the eggs, sausage, and toast, then announce that I'm stepping outside to go explore the grounds. Mom and Niall wave to me, and I'm relieved to escape Elizabeth's withering gaze.

The minute my feet crunch against the gravel outside, I startle the peacocks, and their high-pitched screeching pierces the air. The sound rattles me clear to my bones. The birds peer angrily at me from the treetops, and I quickly change my course. Who knows if they'll charge and peck me to death? I head across the big stretch of grass — the courtyard — until I reach another path that leads to the old rectory I saw from my window.

I button up my coat, and slip in my iPod earbuds, cranking up the volume on an Emilie Autumn song. The cold air makes my breath puff out like white smoke. Behind me, Glenmorrag Castle looms. I can picture the gruesome little gargoyles watching me as I walk.

Soon, the rectory comes into view, and my heart quickens. What clearly used to be a grand arched entrance is now a yawning black mouth, the old gray stone swallowed up by vines and vines of gnarled, twisted ivy. I think it looks sort of beautiful. I've always loved ivy — not least of all because it's my name.

It's not until I duck inside and glance up that I notice the roof isn't really a roof at all. The wood has rotted away, and the entwined ivy has formed a lattice covering. Hazy light and mist filters in between the vines.

"Hello?" I say aloud, and instantly admire the acoustics in the old building. I can't wait to bring my strings in here. I turn off the music on my iPod, and I try the echo out once more. "Helloooo . . ."

"Leave here at once!"

My heart stops. It's that voice from last night. The one I heard as I was falling asleep. I'm sure of it. Adrenaline races through my body, and I look in every dark, shadowy corner but find nothing. Just me, standing in a cavernous, musty rectory more than two centuries old.

Then the ivy moves.

Slowly, the aged boughs begin to untwine and stretch toward me, like long, knobby witch's fingers. I'm certain it must just be a play of the dim light.

Until one lifts a piece of my hair.

I scream.

"Leave this place or you shall die!" the voice says. It's real.

I run straight out of the rectory, and nearly collide with another body. I look up, gasping. I realize how hard I'm trembling.

I see a tall gardener in scruffy brown clothes and boots. Crystal-blue eyes set in a weathered face look curiously at me. His hat sits crooked on his head. He's holding a small shovel, and he has a pair of old gloves stuffed in his pockets.

"What's the hurry, lass?" he asks in a gruff voice.

"In there," I say, catching my breath. "Vines."

Bending his head toward the rectory, he looks inside, and shifts his weight.

"Aye, there's a heap of them in there. Watch yourself. You dunna know what sort of dangers you might encounter at Glenmorrag."

And with that, he turns and disappears around the building, his large rubber boots crunching the dead leaves as he goes.

I turn and look behind me, into the rectory. The ivy vines are back as they were, tightly woven and clinging to the beamless rafters. My heart is pounding, and I'm really starting to think I've lost my mind. The gardener's voice had been too old and deep to be the voice I'd heard moments before.

So *who* is speaking to me? I wonder as I hurry back toward the castle. And why?

Maybe I *should* leave. But where would I go?

There has to be a logical explanation. For a half second I even consider e-mailing Callie about it, but she'd just freak out and insist I keep the webcam on all day, pointed at my room to catch any movement of any sort. She's a total *Ghost Hunters* fan. I'd never hear the end of it.

Besides, there's no such thing as ghosts.

Right?

Chapter 4

☙ NEW FRIENDS ☙

*T*hough I'm on tenterhooks all weekend, there are no more strange voices or noises, and by Sunday night, I'm able to sleep fairly well in my new room. Before I know it, it's Monday morning: my first day of school here in Scotland. I'm not nervous, really — just a little self-conscious.

I stand in front of the mirror in my room, inspecting myself in my new uniform. It consists of a white long-sleeved blouse, a black pullover sweater, a black-and-gray plaid skirt, black tights, and black shoes. Not my style at all.

Mom peeks her head in. "Good morning, sweetie," she says. "Almost ready for breakfast? Oh," she cries when she steps all the way in, "look at you!" She claps. "Are you Gryffindor or Slytherin?"

I sigh. "Slytherin for sure."

Mom laughs. "You look very . . . Scottish, Ivy. And adorable."

I frown at her in the mirror.

Mom crosses the room and pulls me into a hug. "Everything will be okay, sweetie. They'll all love you." She kisses my temple and glances at me in the mirror. "How can they not?"

I smile and pat Mom's arm. "It's okay, Mom. I can handle it if they don't all love me like you do."

She grins. "Just be yourself and you'll be fine."

If only it were that easy.

Niall and Mom drive me to school. I didn't want to have to ride a bus filled with strangers, so I'm glad. Glenmorrag High School is average size, brick, and all one story. It has a huge soccer field — "a football pitch," Niall calls it — that sits off to the side. As Niall comes to a stop in front of the school, I take in the sea of uni-formed kids. The boys wear white shirts with black ties and black sweater-vests, and the girls are in outfits like mine, though some wear pants. Mom was right; I feel like I've arrived at Hogwarts. Too bad this school won't be nearly as fun.

I say good-bye to Mom and Niall and get out of the car. Then I take a deep breath and sling my backpack onto my shoulder, bumping into a girl with long fiery-red curls.

"Och, watch it," she says with a heavy Highland accent. "You nearly took me bloody head off with that thing."

Embarrassed, I give a hesitant smile. "Sorry 'bout that."

Her eyes widen. "Och, an American," she says, and inclines her head. I've come to realize *och* is a standard Scottish exclamation meaning something similar to *oh*. She smiles. "I'm Emma."

"Ivy," I reply. "I'm new."

"Well, Ivy, come on, then. I'll show you to the front office so Headmistress Worley can give you your schedule."

I follow Emma inside, careful not to hurt anyone else with my backpack.

"Where do you live anyway?" Emma asks me as we come to a stop in front of an office door.

"Um . . ." I hesitate a little. "Glenmorrag Castle."

"No way." Emma's eyes again widen. "I've heard that —"

"Okay, Emma, you two might want to hurry along now." A boy our age appears at our side. He's tall and broad-shouldered, with dark hair, silvery eyes, and very white skin. He glances at his watch and raises a dark brow. "Ye dunna want to be late, aye?" He smiles at me, then a little longer at Emma, then walks off to speak to another group of kids.

"Serrus Munro," Emma says, looking after him. Her tongue spins all the *r*'s in his name. "One of the prefects. He's nay too bad."

I watch the group of younger kids disperse the moment Serrus walks up.

"I think I read about prefects in Harry Potter," I admit, feeling childish.

Emma grins. "Oh, yeah. Well, they're kind of like . . . patrolmen. Serrus is our age, a Sixth Year, and he sort of helps keep the younger ones in hand. But he's right." She glances at her watch. "Better go to class. You can go in and see the headmistress. See ya 'round, aye?"

I nod, grateful and relieved. I don't want to get my hopes up, but Emma seems like she could be a friend.

This gives me the confidence to enter the headmistress's office. Ms. Worley is a welcoming middle-aged woman with dark brown hair and green eyes. While I sit in a chair across from her desk, she prints out my schedule and hands me a small map of the school hallways.

"So tell me about yourself, Ivy," she says as she walks me to my first class. She knows all the basics about me — where I'm from, where I'm living now — because Niall enrolled me in the school. "Do you play sports? Music?"

I glance at her. "I play the violin."

She stops and looks at me. "Is that so?"

Smiling, I nod. "Yes, ma'am. Since I was three."

Her eyes light up. "That is marvelous! We have extracurricular music on Thursdays in the afternoon. There's also a grand music festival sponsored by the Strings of the Highlands in the spring. Only the elite are chosen to play, and there's actually a contest for young violinists. Sir Malcolm Catesby will be judging, and the winner will be given a private lesson with him. 'Twould be a great opportunity for anyone looking to advance their music."

Excitement vibrates through me at the thought of playing at the festival, especially in front of Malcolm Catesby — a super-famous violinist.

"Thank you, ma'am," I say. "I look forward to finding out more."

And I mean it. Back home there weren't as many opportunities like this. In fact, my violin teacher in Charleston usually chided me for playing music that was too unconventional, too weird. I wonder if here, people might be more open to something a little strange.

My first class is biology, and the teacher, Mr. MacPherson, is pretty cool. But I have to concentrate hard on his accent to catch everything he says about the parts of a cell.

Emma seems to have appointed herself as my personal tour guide, and finds me in the hallway after class. "Lubly jubly," she says, glancing at my schedule. "We share the next three classes. Come on, then. Off to World History we go." We move into the class and find seats next to each other near the center of the room. "Time to manage the Aztecs."

I don't even mind sitting in class and taking notes — it feels ordinary. Familiar. Like I could almost be back in my old school back home, far from the spooky castle and its eerie voices.

I'm glad to have Emma close by when lunch rolls around. "Let's go grab a sandwich and sit in the Common Room," she suggests. I follow her lead as we make our way to a small, self-serve café. Back in Charleston, Callie and I would be waiting in the long lunch line for mushy mac and cheese. Here, Emma takes a mug of hot tea, an egg-salad sandwich, and a bag of chips. I grab the same, along with some shortbread that looks almost as good as what Jonas brought me the other night. Then we head to the Sixth Years' Common Room and sit at a small table.

"So, Glenmorrag Castle," Emma says, tossing her long red curls over one shoulder. She stirs sugar into her tea. "Your mum married a MacAllister, aye? The laird?"

"Yeah," I answer. I bite into the soft sandwich, which is actually pretty good. "His name is Niall, and he's . . . okay. I've only been here three days." I don't tell her about the spooky goings-on of the weekend. Instead, I tell her about life back in Charleston, and my violin playing. Emma tells me that she has a tin ear when it comes to playing music, but she's also into retro '80s stuff. She's lived in Glenmorrag all her life, and she's an only child, too. I already feel at ease with her.

I'm just thinking about how nice and normal our conversation is compared to my life the past few days when Emma casually asks, "So, seen anything weird at the castle?"

I pause midbite. "Um . . . why do you ask?"

"What's weird besides you, Emma?" a stocky boy asks as he approaches the table. He's joined by a girl who looks like a shorter version of him, with the same wavy brown hair and brown eyes.

Emma rolls her eyes. "Right, you're full of chuckles today, eh, Big D? Ivy, this is Cameron and Derek MacLeod," Emma announces. "They shared a womb."

Fraternal twins. Derek, the boy, flicks Emma on the ear, then smiles at me. "You're the only Yank in the school," he says. "Nice to meet ya."

"You must be Laird MacAllister's stepdaughter," Cameron, the girl, says. "I hear that place is wicked spooky."

"We were just getting to that, isn't that right, Ivy?" Emma urges. "So come on. Anything?"

I squirm, not wanting to sound insane. I can't tell them about the moving vines or my dancing violin. Or that voice. "The castle's . . . dark," I answer. "Not too bad, though."

Now that's an outright lie. I glance at all of them. "Why? What've you heard?"

Emma leans forward, lowering her voice. "My great-auntie, who died many years ago, worked as a maid there once. She swore that rooms turned icy cold, and that things wouldna be where she left them last."

"As in things moved around?" Cameron asks.

"Aye," Emma confirms. "She said her cleaning supplies, which she kept in one specific closet, would disappear and turn up in a strange place, like an upstairs bathtub. She could have sworn there was a dark spirit at work. She also says a young man was murdered there, countless years ago. 'Tis his ghost who haunts, I bet."

I find myself trembling but I try not to let my fear show. I can't believe we're having this conversation. "I hadn't heard anything about that."

Emma regards me. "Never know, Ivy. Keep your eyes peeled."

"So *have* you seen anything?" Cameron asks.

"I have heard *some* things," I answer hesitantly. I'm careful about what I say. I don't want to come off as freakish my first day at school. "Could be the wind, though. It whips through that old castle like something out of a horror movie."

"It's rare that the wind isna roaring in the Highlands," Derek says with a grin. "It can play tricks on ya, though. Dunna let your imagination run wild."

"True," his sister chimes in. She gives me the exact same smile as her brother. "But the Highlands are full o' magic, too. No telling what's going on for real."

"Aye," Emma says, but she's looking at me more seriously than the other two. "No telling at all."

The bell rings, and the twins gather their stuff. They wave to us and head off. As Emma and I gather our book bags, she looks me pointedly in the eye.

"You can tell me," she whispers. "What's really happening in the castle?"

My heart skips a beat. I'm surprised by her insight. "I didn't want to make a big deal in front of everyone," I explain.

"You can trust me," Emma offers. "Swear."

I look at her for several seconds. I have no one else to confide in. No one my own age. I like Emma already. There's a blatant honesty about her that I relate to.

"Okay," I whisper as we walk out of the Common Room. "I know it sounds nuts, but there's this . . . voice. Someone keeps telling me to leave the castle. And," I go on, "there's a heavy, I don't know, *presence* in the air. It's not always there, just sometimes."

"Like what?" Emma asks. Her face is drawn in concern. No mockery at all.

I think. "It feels like someone is watching me. Also, my new step-grandmother isn't the sweetest of old ladies," I add. "I mean, she is in her nineties, but boy, she really doesn't like me."

"Do you think it's her?" Emma asks. "Maybe hissing those things, telling you to leave?" Kids file past us, hurrying to classrooms.

I shake my head. "I'm not sure. It sounds like a guy's voice." I stop and look at Emma. "And . . ." I really hesitate to tell her this.

"Go on," she urges.

"I swear I saw my violin and bow hovering in midair, playing on their own."

I expect Emma to laugh at me but she only nods. "Doesna surprise me one bit. Not after what my auntie told me." She inclines her head. "Doing anything this weekend?" she asks. "We could hang out. Maybe at your place? We could investigate the situation."

A sigh of relief escapes me. "So you don't think I'm crazy?"

"Och," Emma says, heading into our math class. "Of course I think you're crazy." She grins. "But so am I. We'll check it out together. Two is better than one, aye?"

"Definitely," I say.

By the end of the day, Emma and I have exchanged cell numbers and she's urged me to text her if anything else weird happens at the castle. I officially have a friend here. I'm in such a good mood that it takes me a second to notice that it's just Niall picking me up in the car.

"Where's Mom?" I ask, buckling my seat belt.

"She doesna feel so well this afternoon," he answers. "How was school?"

I tell Niall the truth: The first day was better than expected, and Emma, Cam, and Derek seem very nice. Niall looks pleased, and for the first time, things don't seem so awkward between us. Still, the rest of the drive passes without much conversation.

When I get back inside the castle, Mom is sitting on the sofa beside the hearth, covered in a blanket and reading a book.

"You okay?" I ask her, a little worried. Mom rarely gets sick.

She smiles up at me. "Sure, baby, just felt a little off is all. Probably jet lag." She asks me about school, and I fill her in on Emma and the twins, and my classes. This good news seems to perk her up, and when Niall comes into the room, she rises off the couch, telling him she's feeling much better and can accompany him. Apparently, Niall has some land he's interested in up the coast so they're going to check it out. Such is the life of a laird, I guess.

Mom says they will be back before supper and kisses me good-bye. I sling my backpack over my shoulder and head for the kitchen. I'm hoping to say hi to Jonas and maybe get an afternoon snack before settling into my homework upstairs.

But in the shadow of the staircase, I run smack into Elizabeth.

She's watching me. Wordless. Cold eyes. That white-gray bun. I swear she must use a wrench to tighten it.

"Hey," I say, trying to break the ice just a little.

"Good afternoon," she says crisply, correcting me. "You're a MacAllister now, young lady. Behave as one."

I've had about enough. I've not done one thing to this woman, and she hates me. Hates me! I look at her as I walk by her. "I'm not a MacAllister."

"Well, then," Elizabeth says behind me. "If you feel that way, you might be better off locked in the tower."

What?

I stop in my tracks and slowly turn to look at her. Her thin lips rise in a sinister smile. "Aye?"

I turn and hurry away. Not answering, not entertaining her. I don't hear her heels clicking on the floor behind me, so I figure she isn't following. Good. I've had enough of her threats.

The kitchen is empty. "Jonas?" I call. I'm dying to vent to him about my latest encounter with the evil Elizabeth. I set my backpack on the table and head to his room off the kitchen, and lightly knock. No answer.

"Guess he must be out getting groceries or something," I say out loud to no one. I begin to search the cabinets for some crackers, and that's when I notice the big walk-in freezer door is ajar. Thinking Jonas may be inside, I walk to it and open the door wider.

"Jonas?" I call, peering inside.

Suddenly, I'm shoved hard from behind and I fall to the floor of the freezer. The door slams behind me and the lock clicks. My mind whirls. What just happened? I turn and stare blankly at the freezer door. Luckily, there's still a light on in here.

"Hey!" I holler. "Hello? Let me out!"

No one answers. The door remains shut. My heart starts to race.

I try the handle, but it won't budge. The freezer locks from the outside only.

Banging on the door, I yell louder. "Jonas! Elizabeth! I'm in the freezer and I can't get out!" I bang on the door again and again. "Help!"

No one comes. And my cell phone is in my backpack. On the table.

Panic seizes me. Who pushed me? I didn't trip — *something* shoved me. Yet I didn't hear anyone come up behind me. Could it have been Elizabeth? She wanted to lock me in the tower. But I was alone in the kitchen.

Cold sinks in through my school sweater and grips my bones. My lips start to feel numb and I'm shivering. I back into the corner and sit on a big box of lard and wrap my arms around myself. I start cataloging the contents of the freezer, just to keep my mind busy. Three boxes of king crab legs, five boxes of Angus steaks, seventeen bags of chicken breasts . . . my eyes begin to drift shut. I'm so cold, inside and out. . . .

"Miss Ivy! Oh, dear, child, wake up!"

Hands shake my shoulders. I blink and open my eyes. My vision is blurry at first, and it slowly focuses. Jonas is standing over me, worry lines creasing his face. The freezer door is wide open now. I feel a rush of relief.

Over Jonas's shoulder, in the kitchen, I see a movement. There's someone else there. A boy. A boy about my age. Dark, thick wavy hair and a loose white old-fashioned-looking shirt. Our eyes meet, and all I can think is "Wow, he is really cute." But he's frowning fiercely at me. I blink and he's gone.

Or was he ever there?

"Miss Ivy," Jonas pleads. "Can you stand?"

"I think my butt is frozen to the box of lard," I say, and it strikes me as funny. I start to laugh.

"Oh, dear, you're delusional," he answers, and tugs on my elbow. "Come, lass. You need to get warm." I stand,

and Jonas guides me out of the freezer. "However did you trap yourself in here?"

My body is reacting to the change in temperature, and my shivering increases so much I can barely speak. "I — I — I d-d-didn't," I stutter. "S-s-someone p-p-pushed me."

"Come again?" Jonas asks, and he leads me straight to the hearth in the sitting room off the kitchen, where a nice fire is blazing. Jonas drapes a plaid woolen blanket over my shoulders and I sit down, rubbing my arms. Slowly, I start to warm.

"I felt someone shove me," I say again, and look at Jonas. "And then slam and lock the door behind me."

Puzzlement glazes over Jonas's face. He frowns. "The freezer wasn't locked at all, miss. 'Twas unlocked."

I shake my head. "No. I tried the door. It was locked."

Concern etches into Jonas's features. "Yes, miss. I shall look into it. But for now, you stay here and warm yourself by the fire."

I nod, immensely grateful. "And, Jonas? There's no need to tell my mom and Niall about this," I say. "They'll just freak out. I don't know what happened, but I don't want to worry them. Okay?"

Jonas stares at me for several moments. "If I even notice one single sniffle from you, I'll tell them both. I'll not have you coming down with pneumonia, miss."

I nod. "Deal. And thanks, Jonas."

"Of course, young lady. Now let me fix you some tea." He bustles off into the kitchen.

I turn my gaze to the fire, and as I stare at the orange flames, I try to come up with a logical explanation for what's been going on. If I rule out Elizabeth, I can only think of one other thing that could be plaguing me with such malevolence, and I won't lie — it scares me.

It must be a ghost.

The thought is absolutely absurd. But considering what Emma and the twins said at school . . .

If it's not a person who's out to get me, it has to be something supernatural.

I think of the handsome boy I saw in the kitchen moments before. Why was he scowling at me? And why did he disappear as quickly as he'd appeared?

Was *he* the one who had pushed me?

Chapter 5

∽ LOGAN ∼

After two cups of Jonas's steaming tea, I warm up enough to make my way upstairs. I promptly change into my comfy University of South Carolina sweatshirt and pull my hair into a high ponytail. Then I curl up next to the fire but I can't concentrate on homework just yet. I decide to text Emma.

It's cool if you want to come this weekend, but something just happened that might make you change your mind.

It's less than ten seconds before Emma texts me back.

What???

In as few words as possible, I text Emma about my ordeal in the freezer.

Are you freckin' kidding me? she writes back. Are you OK?

I text her back, Yeah, I'm fine. Just freaked out. Then I tell her my ghost theory.

That's what I'd guess it is, she texts back. Well, I'm still coming this weekend. Keep me posted. And just in case, keep a weapon on you at all times.

I want to laugh. Like what? I don't have any weapons!

I've Googled it. If you're dealing with an evil spirit, you need something made of iron. Like a fire poker. That old castle probably has tons of them. Salt works, too. Pinch both and keep them with you.

Pinch?

LOL. You know. Take. Steal. Acquire. Whatever.

OK. Gotcha. Will do.

Good. Now be safe.

I already feel better. Just being able to share the creepy happenings with another person who doesn't think I'm losing my noodles, helps. I even manage to do a little homework before I hear Mom calling me down to supper.

I stay in my sweatshirt, daring Elizabeth to challenge me. I head downstairs, and as I make my way toward the dining room, I stop in front of the gigantic fireplace in the great hall. Glancing over at the hearth, I notice a stand. Just like Emma says, it contains an iron poker, broom, and pan. I grab the poker, weigh it. Not too heavy, but it is long. Glancing around to make sure no one is watching, I take a couple of practice swings. It'll do. I race it quickly back up to my room, set it down by my bed, and tear downstairs, certain Elizabeth will scold me for showing up late to dinner.

But luckily she's not there. Niall says she was feeling poorly so will be taking supper in her room. Phew. Mom seems tired, but she tells me about her and Niall's drive to the coast and asks me more questions about school. I feel a little guilty not telling her about the freezer incident, but I know she and Niall would think I was going crazy — especially if I told them I suspected a cruel ghost was to blame.

When supper is over, I go back upstairs. My poker is still beside my bed, and I feel safer with it there. I get my violin and bow, and despite the cold, crack open the window, nestle into the plush cushion on the seat, and play. I continue the haunting melody I started my first day here. The brine of the sea mixes with the fresh scent of the Highlands as I throw myself into my music, and I'm able to forget, even for just a moment, that a spirit of some sort is trying to scare me out of Glenmorrag Castle. Being here, in this strange new place, has awakened an inspiration inside of me that is stronger than ever before. I compose and play until my fingers are stiff and my eyes become too heavy to hold open.

I fall asleep there by the window, my head resting against the stone wall, and my violin in my lap.

All at once, I startle awake. A heartbreaking melody — played by a flute — reaches my ears. It's very distant, almost a whisper, and I cock my head to determine where it might be coming from. Someone's stereo? A TV? I have to remind myself that I'm the only person staying on the third floor.

The digital clock on my bedside table reads two A.M. The faint sound of the flute continues, and without much thought at all, I grab my poker and leave the room in search of it. I creep down to the first floor. Once I enter the great hall, I stop and listen. It's dark, and cold. Perhaps one of the staff left music on in the kitchen?

But as soon as I enter the kitchen, the music stops.

I stand for several minutes, frustrated, looking around. One light burns at the double stove. I trail my hand along the long butcher-block counter in the center of the room. I think about waking Jonas but I decide to leave him alone. I've given him enough of a scare today.

I blow on a long wisp of pink hair that has eluded my ponytail. If I'm here, I might as well have a snack. I set my poker on the counter, and open the fridge. I grab the milk. I smile, knowing Elizabeth would croak if she saw me. I unscrew the lid, lift it to my mouth, and take several long swallows.

All at once, the hairs rise on the back of my neck and my skin tingles. I turn completely around.

My breath catches in my throat, which sends me into a coughing fit. I almost drop the whole container. But my eyes will not leave the vision before me. I can do nothing but helplessly stare.

It — he — can't be real.

The boy that I saw standing in the kitchen earlier is here. Before me. He looks to be about seventeen or eighteen, with rich, dark brown hair. He has the oddest mercury-colored eyes. He wears a white shirt with billowy long sleeves and dark-colored pants, laced in the front and tucked into knee-high worn leather boots. He seems a bit smoky and wavy — almost see-through but not quite.

He is just as attractive as before . . . but he must be who's been talking to me. And who shoved me into the freezer.

He's the ghost.

I can't speak — my mouth won't even move — so I do nothing more than gape. Fright grips my throat, forces adrenaline to thump through me. I glance over at my iron poker. I need to get it. I shouldn't have let it out of my grasp.

"That thing willna hurt me, foolish girl," he laughs wickedly. "I warned you before to leave," he adds, his brows furrowed. "You and your mother are no' welcome here." He suddenly moves, closing the gap between us. "You must leave, before one or both o' you get hurt!" His intense gaze meets my frightened one, and for a moment, he simply searches my face. I can't speak, and it takes every effort on my part to continue breathing. Then he brings his mouth close to my ear. Close, but not touching.

"Leave Glenmorrag Castle whilst you still can," he warns. "It is no' safe here. Especially for you."

A shiver runs through my body.

Then he draws back, and as I stand staring into his

mesmerizing eyes, he simply vanishes. Straight into thin air. Gone.

I stand perfectly still for a long time before I pull in a large breath. Finally, my voice returns.

"Hello?" I whisper. I step forward and wave my hand through the area the boy just stood in. There's not one scrap of evidence that proves what just happened really truly had happened. No sound, no flute, no voice, no boy.

I hastily put the milk back in the fridge, grab my poker, and run back upstairs, skidding in my oversized socks. I hurl myself into my room, throw the latch, and bolt the lock. I run to my window seat spot, tuck the poker beside me, and pull my knees up. Leaning my head against the stone, I wrap my arms around myself and stare out into the night.

It's clear that I need to alter my thinking. Ghosts *do* exist. And they aren't weightless apparitions that drift around looking like white sheets with little holes cut out for eyes. They aren't orbs of light that may or may not be a dust ball when captured on a digital camera. They're as they had been in life, only their bodies aren't solid anymore. At least, I think.

I want — no, *need* — to figure out who this ghost is, and why he's haunting me. Maybe someone at Glenmorrag knows something about him — his name, or who he is. Who he was.

But I'm most determined to figure out why he wants me gone.

I spend the remainder of the night curled up on the window seat, and even manage to get a little sleep before morning. The moment my eyes open, my thoughts are on the ghost boy I saw in the kitchen.

I know what I need to do. I hurry through a shower and throw on my uniform. I'm not the least bit hungry for breakfast, but I know if I skip it, Mom will chide me about the "most important meal of the day." So I hasten to the dining room and eat a bowl of porridge — thin oatmeal that really is tasty after I dump a load of butter, sugar, and cream into it.

"Why the rush today, Ivy?" asks Mom. I glance across the table. Elizabeth is watching me with her icy eyes, and again, I'm pretty sure I see them shift a little in size. So freaky.

I quickly return my attention to Mom. "There's just something I need to do before Niall drives me to school,"

I answer. "Can you please tell him I'll meet him outside the castle doors in about fifteen minutes?" Before she or Elizabeth can protest, I slide out of my chair and scamper into the kitchen.

I can't believe I was here last night, face-to-face with the handsome ghost who spoke to me. Thankfully, there is no sign of him this morning, and Jonas is there, examining the shelves and making inventory notes.

I lean against the counter. "I have a question, Jonas." He looks at me, waiting. "Do you know of any ghosts at Glenmorrag?"

One corner of his mouth lifts and he answers after a minute.

"I do say, Miss Ivy, I was wondering when you'd be inquiring about such. Especially since you nearly caught him yesterday after what happened in the freezer." He shakes his head. "Still haven't deciphered that one yet."

My heart stops. "So you know about him!" I exclaim. "What haven't you deciphered about the freezer? He's the one who pushed me in, right?"

"Nay," Jonas says with confidence. "He's the one who found me and hurried me to help you."

This shocks me. I don't know if I believe that.

"You should find Ian Murray — the gardener — and speak to him," Jonas adds. "He'll be in the hedge maze, I reckon. He knows the boy better than I." He leans closer. "I daresay if the lad has shown himself to you, 'tis an interest you spark in him."

"A terrible interest," I answer. "He's been trying to scare me away from Glenmorrag."

Jonas studies me. "All the same, speak to Ian. He can tell you what you need to know."

I thank Jonas, then head outside, tossing on my coat and hat. I'm on a mission. I find Ian in the back, trimming the ancient hedge maze. Or rather, I hear him, the blades of the shears zinging together as they clip. I'm hopeful that he'll give me some real information.

I enter the head-high dark green maze, the frosty wind biting my cheeks and nose. It feels like a different world in here, surrounded by the tall bushes. The sky above is dramatic in a way that I'm realizing is uniquely Scottish: gray and white, with a streak of clear blue and another of bold pink.

I follow the sound of the shears until I see Ian's head above the next hedge over, and I clear my throat and call out. The last thing I want to do is startle a six-foot gardener with a pair of sharp hedge shears.

"Mr. Murray?" I say, trying not to let my anxiety show. "Mr. Murray — it's Ivy."

Suddenly, the shears stop, and for a few seconds, there's silence. "Take the next left, lass," he says, his voice gravelly and heavily accented. I do as he says, and find myself next to him. He looks down at me, his face expressionless. A cigarette dangles from his lips. "Aye?"

I shift my weight, draw a deep breath, and try to look sane. "This is going to sound crazy," I begin, giving a nervous laugh. "Jonas told me to talk to you about the — the ghost here at Glenmorrag?" I eye him. "The boy?"

Ian Murray stares at me for a long time. His expression is unreadable as he pulls long on his cigarette. Finally, I can take no more. I have to get to school.

"Never mind," I say, and start to walk away. I take about five steps.

"He's shown himself to you, then?"

I stop and turn, seeing a hint of amusement in his gaze. That's when I decide I like Ian Murray. I sigh a quiet breath of relief. "Yes. He has."

Ian Murray throws his cigarette down and crushes it with his boot. "Och, but that didna take long," he mutters, chuckling. "He must fancy you."

Fancy me? That would mean that the ghost *likes* me, which doesn't seem to be the case.

"Well, he's got a funny way of showing it," I respond, my heart racing. "He keeps trying to scare me away, and he's doing a good job of it. Do you know his name?" I ask.

Ian grins, then hooks the shears by the handles over one forearm. "Logan Munro."

"Logan," I mutter. I can hardly believe I'm saying the name of a *ghost*, who I've actually met in person. Sort of, anyway.

I look at Ian. "So he's . . . real?"

Ian nods. "Been here at Glenmorrag for as long as I can recall." He cocks his head and scratches beneath the brim of his cap. "One can often hear him playing his flute. He was a musician in life, I believe." Ian pauses. "So he spoke to you, lass? Tried to scare you off?"

Logan's angry, beautiful face comes to mind, and I nod. "Yes, and he was . . . super mad."

Ian thinks a moment. "Do you wish to speak to him again?"

I don't even hesitate. "Yes," I say quietly. "I do."

"Right. Then all you have to do is call his name. If he wants to visit with you, he'll appear. If no', then, well" — he gives a half-cocked grin — "he simply won't. A mind of his own, that lad."

I search Ian's face. "Am I going insane?"

Ian barks out a laugh. "Nay, young miss. 'Twould be natural to think you are seeing things. But the lad can only show himself to those who actually believe in spirits. And, you're in the Highlands now, gell." It takes me a second to realize *gell* — with a hard *g* — means *girl*. Ian looks at me a minute before adding, " 'Tis a mystical place filled with enchantment."

I peek down at the space between my feet, a little embarrassed. "Do . . . you know anything more about him? Like why he might want me gone?" I glance up, chewing on my lip and waiting for an answer.

Ian lets out a long sigh. "Well, that I dunna know. Logan is a somewhat mysterious lad. I'd guess he lived here about two hundred years ago, but he doesna remember why or when he came to the castle. I myself suspect he may have been murdered, the poor soul. That's why his spirit cannot rest, why he roams the castle grounds.

Legend has it that if a ghost's murder is solved, he can then finally rest in peace." Ian looks sad and thoughtful. "Mayhap the lad will tell you more himself. That is, if he fancies to."

The talk of murder has me trembling a little. This castle has so many secrets. I glance over my shoulder, knowing Niall must be waiting for me.

"Do the MacAllisters, uh, have they seen him?" I ask.

Ian Murray slowly shakes his head. "Nay. The laird knew of him when he was a wee lad, but at some point" — Ian shrugs again — "he grew up and stopped believing."

I think that's pretty sad. "What about Elizabeth MacAllister?" I whisper.

A stony expression crosses Ian's face. "I'm no' sure, but I suspect that even if she did believe, young Logan wouldna show himself to her."

I bob my head in understanding. I probably wouldn't show myself to her, either, if I could help it. "Okay. Thanks, Mr. Murray."

"Ian," he says with a kind smile.

I smile back. "Ian."

He continues his hedge trimming, and I turn and make my way out of the maze.

Chapter 6

ENCOUNTERS

As Niall drives me to school, I think about what Ian had said, about Logan showing himself only to those who believe in ghosts. When did I begin believing in ghosts? It must be a new development.

I look over at Niall, thinking about him growing up at the castle. Seeing Logan as a child, but not believing in spirits anymore. How would he forget something like seeing a ghost? I wonder what Mom would think. I'm not going to worry her with it now, though. But I will tell Emma everything. Maybe she'll be able to help me figure out why Logan Munro is haunting me, and how I can either get him to stop, or send him back to . . . wherever he came from.

However, at school, I can never get Emma alone. Our teachers watch us like hawks so there's no time to whisper or pass notes in class, and during lunch, we're joined by the twins. I decide I'll just text my friend later, or wait to reveal everything when she comes to the castle over the weekend.

Mom is the one to pick me up from school, which is a nice surprise. She drives us to the village to pick up fish-and-chips for dinner. She's still getting used to driving on the left side of the road, and the adventure of that finally takes my mind off of Logan for a few minutes. By the time we make it into the village of Glenmorrag, I'm a little dizzy.

"Now that was fun, huh?" Mom says, laughing and shaking her head. She glances out the windshield and gasps. "Wow, Ivy — would you look at this place!"

We both step out of the Rover, and I take in the sight.

The daylight is waning, and Glenmorrag Village looks like something out of a movie. It's still a walled township like it was in medieval times, and we walk through a guard post in the old wall. I half expect to see a dirt-smudged thief with his head and arms poking out of the stocks, and people throwing rotted heads of cabbage at him. We walk along the cobbled streets, past a couple of touristy shops, and find the chip shop — a one-room establishment. There're no seats inside, and the two grizzled old ladies behind the counter fry the fish and French fries (aka "the chips"). They squirt vinegar and some weird-looking brown sauce all over them, then wrap them up for us in thick white paper.

"Let's eat ours here," Mom suggests. "We'll take Niall his."

"Sure," I agree, and we find a place to sit outside, on a concrete bench facing the sea. I stare down at my food, feeling slightly dubious.

"I promise, sweetheart. You're going to love it," Mom says. She breaks off a piece of fish and pops it into her mouth. I do the same. The crispy fried batter and vinegar, and even the unknown brown sauce, are totally delicious.

"You're right," I admit. "It's great."

Mom studies me for a moment. "I understand how this is all probably so overwhelming, Ivy," she says seriously. "I love Niall, you know." She brushes her hand over mine. "I never thought I'd find that after your dad. He loved me so . . . completely. Just like he loved you." I nod, feeling choked up. Mom glances out over the sea for a moment, then turns her gaze to me. "I guess I've been ignoring you a little lately, and I don't mean to. I haven't been feeling totally well the past few days. I'm sorry, baby."

I smile at my mom. Her acknowledgment really does make me feel better.

"It's okay, Mom," I assure her. "I want you to rest if you're sick, and I'm glad you're happy with Niall."

Mom studies me. "Niall hasn't exactly acquired the knack for communicating with a teenage girl yet, I'm afraid. But I know he wants to." She smiles. "He tells me he feels like a fool for not knowing what to say to you."

That, too, makes me feel better.

"Well, I don't exactly know what to say to him, so maybe we can learn together," I answer.

Mom's face brightens. "That'd be wonderful, sweetheart."

The drive back to the castle is just as terrifying as the drive to the village, with Mom gripping the Rover's wheel so hard that her knuckles are white. Thankfully, we make it back in one piece.

As we get out of the car, a peacock's scream rips through the air, startling me. I suck in a breath, shoving my hands deep into my coat pockets. Something makes me look up, toward the castle's far end facing the sea. I find my room quickly, and freeze.

Someone stands at the window, looking down.

Directly at me.

I narrow my eyes, trying to make out who it is, but before I can, the figure moves aside. Who's in my room? Was it a maid? Are they stripping the beds and washing linens today? I keep forgetting that I'm supposed to allow the elderly housekeeper, Mrs. Willets, and Trudy, the young maid who spoke to me on my first morning here, to take care of it. Habit, I suppose. I've never had a maid before, and to be honest, I don't want one now. I'd rather have a room with total privacy than someone coming in and going through my stuff.

Maybe it was Elizabeth I saw in the window, though. Or was it Logan?

Who is — or was — he? Why does he want me to leave? Why would it not be safe here? I can't stop the questions from racing through my mind.

Mom brings Niall his fish-and-chips — I suppose Elizabeth will be dining alone tonight, which is great news — and I head straight up to my room. While I'm not exactly scared, I am a little apprehensive. I draw a long, deep breath and open my door.

A cold shiver races through my body.

Not only is my violin hovering in midair, the bow poised over the strings as though someone unseen is holding it, but my laptop and my iPod are also floating. My clothes are firing out of my drawers, one garment at a time; my schoolbooks on my desk are open, pages flipping back and forth. I stare in horror, gaping. This is not okay — I have to do something. I stride into my room and stand directly beneath my instrument. Just as I reach out to grasp the base, it drops, and I catch it with a gasp. My bow clamors to the floor.

I find myself angry. I grab my laptop and my iPod from the air and set them on the bed, and carefully load my violin back into its case.

"You know, this instrument is special to me," I shout to my empty room, snapping the case shut. Anger and fear are making me shake inside. "How would you feel if I snapped your precious flute in two? You can at least have the courtesy of showing yourself if you're going to toss my strings and belongings around." I prop my case against the wall where I'd had it before. "Or how about you just don't touch my stuff at all."

Everything stops. Clothes drop, pages stop flipping. It is totally silent, and the longer I stand there, the madder I become.

"Logan," I say out loud, furious. "I'm not leaving Glenmorrag. I don't have anywhere else to go anyway. You can't scare me off. So you might as well stop with all the tricks. Seriously. Not cool."

Of course, there's no response.

Frustrated, I sink down on the bed, my head in my hands. I almost want to cry. When I lift my head, Logan is there. My breath catches.

He's standing propped against one of the columns of my bed. He looks exactly the same as before, and even though I've been expecting him, I'm still taken aback by his presence.

"What do you mean, you won't leave?" he demands. "You've no choice. You're no' wanted here, gell."

"By who?" I demand. I stare at him. He looks so . . . real. "You? Elizabeth? I'm only sixteen. I can't just . . . leave. This is where I live now. Why do you want me to go so badly?"

He frowns. "Are you daft, gell? I've already told ya — this place isn't safe." He leans forward. "Go!"

I squeeze my eyes shut but then I open them. I frown back. "No."

Logan mutters what must be a Gaelic swear under his breath and disappears.

Blinking, I scan the room. "Logan? Where'd you go?"

Silence.

"Ugh!" I grumble in frustration, and fling myself against my pillow.

I want to get up and text Emma. I have homework to do, too. But the events of the past few days, combined with the still-lingering jet lag, make me suddenly tired to my bones.

I'm just drifting off to sleep when I hear a strange noise. Footsteps. Fast, harsh little heel taps against the hardwood, rushing past my room. I'll bet anything it's Elizabeth, snooping around. But in the middle of the night?

I roll out of bed, cross to the door, and poke my head out. The corridor is empty. I shut my door, then throw the dead bolt.

I go back to sleep, and I dream of objects in my room — my hairbrush, my iPod, my All Stars — floating above me and of Logan watching me through the drapes around my bed. I dream of mist and wind and rain.

When a weak stream of light filters into my room the next morning, I feel like I haven't slept at all. I'm itching to compose — a new piece has burrowed into my brain in the night — but I have to get ready for school. I promise myself I'll work on the new piece in the evening — provided Logan leaves me alone. Plus, tomorrow will be the after-school music program Headmistress Worley mentioned. And I haven't forgotten about the Strings of the Highlands festival and contest.

The rest of the week passes in a blur — but without any sign of Logan or any objects in my room being disturbed. The after-school music program is fun — Cam is in it, since she plays the piano, and the school's big music room is a good place to practice my strings. Still, I prefer to play at home. Every night after school, I play my new composition on my window seat. It's coming together nicely — it's spooky, sorrowful, with just a twinge of punk. I know I have this dimly lit, cold castle and my frustration with a ghost to thank for my inspiration.

Although I eat lunch with Emma and the twins every day, I don't say anything at all about Logan, preferring to wait until I'm alone with Emma at the castle on Saturday afternoon. I feel some of my anxiety settle just knowing I'll have decent company then.

Finally, it's the weekend. As soon as Emma steps inside the foyer of the castle, I practically pounce on her and drag her into the library on the first floor. That's where I've been hanging out since breakfast, practicing violin. Mom and Niall have gone into the village and Elizabeth, thankfully, is nowhere to be found.

"This place," Emma says, grinning and looking around in wonder, "is positively wicked. I've seen it from far away, of course, but never inside." She turns and looks at me. "What's it like sleeping in a haunted castle? Pretty creepy, I bet."

"Try waking up to your clothes flying all over the room," I answer, shutting the library door. "Yeah, I'd say it has its quirks."

Emma's eyes widen with curiosity. "You didn't tell me about that!" she gasps.

"Patience," I tell her. We sit together on the sofa by the crackling fire, and in whispers, I fill her in on everything: my encounters with the handsome ghost, his paranormal tricks, what Ian said about him being murdered.

When I'm done, Emma shakes her head, those fiery-red spirals bouncing. "We've got to figure this ghostly lad out, Ivy. It's true that it could be he was killed before his time, and that's why he's hanging about."

I shrug. "I tried talking to him the other night, but he's so stubborn."

Emma frowns. "Och, girl. Be careful about confronting the ghost. He could be dangerous."

"I'm not sure he is," I admit, feeling confused. "Oh, and I keep calling him 'the ghost,' but he has a name. Logan Munro. According to Ian, he's haunted this castle for a while —"

"His name is Munro?" Emma interrupts. "Remember Serrus, the prefect you met on your first morning? We should tell him about Logan. He might know something."

I do remember the good-looking prefect but I'm puzzled. "Why would Serrus know something?"

Emma smiles. "Because, lass," she says, "he's a Munro."

My heart quickens. "No way." I hadn't paid attention to his last name when we first met.

Emma smiles. "Way. And he has a bunch of cousins nearby, also with the last name Munro. Big lads." She holds her hand way above her head. "We'll find him on Monday."

Could this Serrus guy be related to Logan? Might he know something about his death? Now that I think about it, Serrus did have a flash of silver in his eyes, somewhat similar to Logan's. I'll have to wait to find out.

Emma notices my violin and raises an eyebrow. "Would you mind playing for me?" she asks, sounding uncharacteristically shy.

"Of course!" I say, flattered that she asked. I pick up my violin and carefully play the melody I've been working on.

When I'm done, I set down my instrument, flushed and energized.

Emma applauds, her eyes shining. "Brilliant!" Her voice resonates through the library. "Your playing is absolute magic, Ivy Calhoun."

I blush, ducking my head.

"Thanks," I tell Emma as I set my strings on my lap. "My music is like one of my appendages. A part of me."

Emma grins. "I can tell."

Just then, Jonas appears at the doorway with a large tray of egg-salad sandwiches, two glasses with a few chunks of ice in each, and two cans of Coke. A pile of fresh shortbread, half-dipped in chocolate, rests on the side. He sets it down and says, "'Tis a rather interesting tune you play, young Ivy. Quite impressive."

I blush again, thank him, and introduce Emma.

Jonas gives a short nod. "Young lady, welcome to the grim halls of Glenmorrag. I hope you enjoy your visit. Good day."

"Cool guy," Emma says after Jonas has left and we dig into our food. "So, you feel like having company here at the castle on Halloween? It falls on Wednesday this year, which sucks, but oh well. What do you say?" She grins mischievously. "I'll bring Derek and Cam. They're dying to see this place."

I laugh. "Sure," I say. "I'll have to clear it with my mom and stepdad first. Since it's a school night." I hope Mom and Niall say yes. I like the idea of having more friends over. And I don't really relish the idea of being alone here, with Logan roaming about, on Halloween.

After we finish eating, I give Emma the tour of the castle. I show her the suit of armor, the sitting room, the kitchen, and the gargoyles. All of it fascinates her. Finally, I bring her up to my room on the third floor.

Emma peeks inside. "You dunna get scared at night in here, all alone?"

"It's unnerving," I answer. "But now that I've seen Logan face-to-face, it's not as creepy as before. Now at least I know who's been messing with me." I glance at her over my shoulder. "Wanna see the rectory?"

I've been itching to try out my violin in there, and I'd prefer to have someone with me in case the ivy vines decide to attack again.

"That'd be sweet," she answers.

We head downstairs, where we retrieve our raincoats from the foyer closet. Just as I'm zipping mine up and pulling on the hood, I feel a presence.

A human presence.

"Where are you going?"

I spin around, and stare into the piercing eyes of Elizabeth MacAllister. Her mouth is pulled so tight that her lips are nothing more than a thin red line.

I nod to the front door. "Outside," I say. "With my friend Emma. Emma, this is Lady MacAllister."

Elizabeth slowly turns her frosty gaze on Emma. She says nothing, and I notice her grasping the giant ruby ring she wears and twisting it around her bony little finger. Its size is really almost gaudy.

"Pleasure," Emma says, and I already know I'll get an earful once we're outside.

Elizabeth studies me hard for several seconds, noting my violin case strapped over my shoulder. "I see you'll be playing that instrument." Her gaze lifts. "Do make sure you keep that noise away from the main hall. Or I'll have to take it away from you."

And with that, she walks away. Fast little heels clicking, back ramrod straight.

"Noise? Is she blooming daft?" Emma spits.

I watch Elizabeth until she disappears, a frown pulling at my mouth. "I'd like to see her take it away. I have half a mind to play as screeching and horribly as I can right next to her until her hair pops out of that tight bun," I mutter.

Emma laughs. "I'll give you ten pounds if you do it."

That makes me laugh, too. At that moment, Mom and Niall walk in the door, shaking the rain off the big black umbrella they were sharing.

"Ivy, introduce us!" Mom calls out. She's looking really pale, and I wonder if she heard what Elizabeth said to me.

"Mom, are you feeling okay?" I ask. She waves me off. "Sorry," I say. "Emma, this is my mom, Julia, and my, um, stepfather . . . Niall, Laird MacAllister," I say, stumbling over the words.

Niall extends his hand and shakes Emma's. "Nice of you to visit, Emma."

"Oh, yes! Ivy was so pleased to make a lovely friend like you," Mom says.

"Aye," Emma responds. "We sort of just clicked after she nearly clobbered me with her backpack."

Mom and Niall chuckle, and Mom announces that she's starving, so they're going to ask Jonas for lunch. Emma and I wave to them and head outside.

It's only slightly drizzly now as we walk briskly toward the rectory. I've learned that drizzle can turn into downpour in the blink of an eye, but I really want to try out the rectory's acoustics.

"Nice folks," Emma says. "Your grandmother is a complete loon, though."

I groan. "Tell me about it. And she's definitely not my grandmother," I clarify. "I can't figure out why she hates me so much."

"I think she already hates me as well," Emma adds as

we make our way to the path leading to the sea. "Maybe she just hates young people."

Could be.

As we near the rectory, I turn to my friend. "Emma? Why do you believe in ghosts?"

She gives me a half smile. "My da was in the Royal Highland Fusiliers," she begins. "Like the army," she explains. "He commanded an infantry platoon and charged an enemy ambush three times to rescue a fellow injured soldier." She looks at me. "His fellow made it. But my da didn't. I was only nine at the time. I talk to him, especially when I'm really missing him." She looks wistful. "He doesna talk back, and he doesna appear to me, but I feel him there, listening."

"Wow," I say, holding her gaze. "No wonder we clicked so fast. My dad died, too. I was thirteen. He had cancer." I swallow hard.

"Sisters at heart, then," Emma says. She links her arm through mine. "We'll figure this out, Ivy. I promise."

We're at the rectory, and I lead Emma inside. The airy chamber is cavernous, shadowy, and smells of clover and wet, freshly cut grass and damp earth. Thankfully, the ivy vines are still and peaceful. For now.

"Wow," Emma says, looking around. "You play in here, do ya?"

"Well, I'd like to," I answer. "The acoustics are sick."

"I bet," she agrees. "Would make your tunes even more wicked."

I smile at her. "I'm actually thinking of entering the Strings of the Highlands festival," I admit. "There's a contest. So says Headmistress Worley."

Emma grins. "I think you should do it." Then she glances at her phone and sees the time. "Och, I'm sorry, Ivy, but I'd best be on my way," she says. "I promised my mum we'd have supper together. You can come to my house next. Mum would love to meet you."

I'm disappointed she's going, but I nod. "Sounds like a plan."

I walk Emma back to the front of the castle, where she's parked her scooter. As she straddles the machine and tugs on her helmet, she peers at me.

"If you see anything else at all, call or text," she says. She starts up her scooter, and the low purr bounces off the stone walls of Glenmorrag. She points at me. "I mean it, Ivy. Dunna hold out on me."

I laugh. "Promise."

I watch Emma ramble along the gravel path until she's out of sight, then I head back to the rectory. I'm a little hesitant to step inside alone, but I make myself. No sense being a scaredy-cat.

"I warned you tae leave!"

Logan Munro is striding toward me, and I back against the ivy-covered stone wall. My throat constricts, and I can't say a word. I expected him, yet I didn't. I simply stare.

"And now you've brought another gell here? Are you daft? Did you no' hear me when I said this place wasna safe? No matter your new father is the laird — I want you tae leave. You've no business here."

My temper flares. "You don't tell me where my business is!" I snap. "As I said before, I'm staying. So you'd better get used to sharing this big old castle with me!" I edge around him, hands on hips. I think about what Ian said, about Logan not knowing why he's stuck here. "You know," I add vehemently, "instead of being so pigheaded and mean, why don't you just chill out, Logan Munro? I could help you, you know? Find out what happened to you? Figure out why you're still here after all these years?" I wave my hand in the air. "But who am I kidding? You're too busy being a bully to accept any help from me. Too busy shoving me into the freezer." I exhale — hard.

Logan stares at me with a mystified look on his face.

We are at a stalemate for several moments.

"I didna push you into that freezer," he says. "And I dunna need any help. From you or anyone else."

"Why not?" I ask. "Ian Murray says you don't remember anything about, well, your —"

"My death?" Logan says with a little sarcasm. "Nay, I remember nothing at all. But it must not've been my time to go, otherwise I wouldna be here." He looks at me, silver eyes blazing. "There's nothing that you, a wee gell from another time and another land, can do to help me."

I frown at him. "You don't know me. You don't know what I can do. But," I continue, "I do know what *you* can do. And I want you to stop it. It's not working anymore. So just . . . quit."

Logan Munro stares at me and blinks.

Then, with a nod, he disappears.

Chapter 7

∽ FAIRY TALE ∾

I head back to the castle, my emotions roiling, and my desire to compose extinguished. I didn't think I'd ever get into a fight with a ghost, but my life is proving to be more and more surprising.

Up in my room, I open my laptop and decide to see what I can find out about Logan on the Internet. Turns out, not much. Searching *Logan Munro* just brings up a bunch of modern-day people named Logan Munro, and most of them not even in Scotland.

I suddenly wish for my dad. I miss him so much. I look at the framed photo of him I've placed on my bedside table. If ghosts can exist, I wonder, why didn't Dad try to contact me? To find me? Is it because he wasn't taken too abruptly? He'd been sick for a long time, and he'd put all his affairs in order before he passed. There was nothing for him to resolve. I swallow hard.

Logan said his death happened before his time. Was it really murder? And if so, who killed him? And why?

I sleep badly that night, dreaming of nonsensical things: talking hedge trimmers, icy-blue eyes that float around the castle, staring at me, following me.

Then, sometime in the night, something bolts me out of sleep.

I can't breathe.

I sit up, coughing, pulling at the neck of my T-shirt. Scrambling out of bed, I continue to cough, tears rolling from my eyes. It feels like something is choking me, but nothing is there. The lights flicker on, then off, and the room grows icy cold. Adrenaline rushes through me.

"Help!" I let out a strangled cry as I reach for the door. "Someone help —"

And just as suddenly, the feeling of invisible fingers against my throat passes. I slump to the ground, gasping for air. I wonder if anyone heard me cry out, but the castle remains silent and sleeping. Eventually, my fear subsides and I'm able to crawl back into bed, but I leave the lights on.

Apparently ghosts *can* hurt people after all. And they can lie, too. I am enraged.

The next morning, instead of going down to breakfast, I grab my raincoat and rubber boots to go for a walk in the light rain. Maybe the cold Highland air will soothe me. I walk along the edge of the seawall, and let the chilly drops patter against my face until my cheeks grow numb. I walk, think, and listen to music. Logan might be easy on the eyes, but I've had about enough of his interference in my life. I could have been seriously hurt last night. If I can solve the mystery of his death, maybe that will make him go away. It seems like the easiest solution.

My thoughts are swirling. When I get back to the castle, I want to escape up to my room, but Mom calls me into the sitting room.

"There you are, sweetie!" she exclaims. "I have something to tell you — I can't keep it in any longer!" She grasps my hand, kisses my cheek, and pulls me to stand next to Niall, who has risen from his seat. I chance a quick peek at Grandmother Elizabeth, silent in the corner.

"We have an announcement to make!" Mom says excitedly, and links her arm through her husband's. A twinkle flashes in her eyes.

"Aye, well," Niall says, and his gaze rests on mine for a nanosecond. "It looks as though the MacAllister family will grow by one more, come the spring." He pulls Mom close and kisses the top of her head.

I blink. What?

A sound — not exactly a gasp, but more like a . . . gurgle — erupts from old Elizabeth. I'm tempted to make the same sound.

Mom smiles at me. "We're having a baby! Ivy, you're going to be a big sister!"

Surprise has me so choked up, I can't even reply. My gaze bounces between my mom and Niall. Mom's smile cracks her entire face in two, and she anxiously awaits my reaction. No wonder she's been pale and feeling "off" lately.

"Wow," I say, totally staggered by the announcement but trying not to look like an idiot. Or a party pooper. "Mom, Niall — that's great!" I move to hug my mom, but she beats me to it and embraces me so tightly my hat is pushed off my head.

Over Mom's shoulder, I peer at Elizabeth MacAllister. Her eyes are locked tightly onto mine. Her face grows redder and redder and she keeps twisting that ruby ring around her finger.

Suddenly, Niall sweeps his grandmother into his embrace. "So, Gran, what do you think? You're goin' tae have a great-grandchild of MacAllister blood," he says, kissing her cheek. He pulls back and looks at her. "Can you stand another MacAllister running about the place?" he asks.

"Any babe of yours, my love, is welcome here at Glenmorrag," she says, but her stony expression implies otherwise. Then she looks directly at me. My insides freeze.

"Come on, Ivy!" Mom says, putting her arm around my shoulder. "Let's go into the village and shop. Just us girls."

It would do me good to get out of this castle for a bit with everything that's happened. I agree, and Mom and I leave before Elizabeth can say anything.

In the car, I almost open up to my mom about Elizabeth's hateful looks. I almost tell her about Logan and how I'd been choked last night. But I don't want to stress her out. Especially not now. I can't believe she's really going to have a baby. Me, a big sister at sixteen?

We make it into town okay, even with Mom's erratic driving. There, we stroll over the cobblestones, window-shopping. Mom loops her arm through mine and pulls me close.

"So, what do you *really* think about the baby?" she asks.

I pat her hand. "I think it's great, Mom," I answer. "I'm a little shell-shocked, but I'll get used to it."

Mom beams. "I can't believe it, Ivy. I never thought it would happen again. Any of this, really. It's like a fairy tale."

For Mom, it truly is. For me? I'm not sure what to call my experience in Scotland so far. Not a fairy tale, but a horror story of some kind? Or a mix thereof?

On our stroll, we pass the library, and I convince Mom to stop in. What better place to research Logan?

Leaving Mom at the section of new parenting books, I cross the small, plaid-covered atrium and make my way to the reference desk. The scent of old leather and older paper permeates the place. I like it. A young librarian wearing a brown sweater and a yellow-and-orange plaid scarf sits staring at her computer screen.

"Can I help you?" she asks, her *you* sounding more like *yooh* — an accent that's almost familiar to me by now.

"I'm trying to find some information about someone from around here who died about two hundred years ago," I whisper. "It might have been an accident . . . or a murder."

The librarian points over her shoulder. "It'd be in Glenmorrag history books." She inclines her head. "Just in that wee section over there. Not that hefty, I fear. You can also try the census books. They're in that room, with the computer. Let me know if you need any help."

"Thanks," I respond, and I head off to investigate.

I scan the small amount of books on the shelves about Glenmorrag history, but none seems that helpful. Then I check a few of the census books in the 1700s and 1800s range. In the one dated 1750–1850, I happen upon Logan's name.

My heart leaps. *Logan Munro, born to Mirrah Munro, in the year of our God and Savior, eighteen hundred and thirty-three.*

That's all it says. Still, it's a start.

After we return from town, Mom goes to her room for a nap, and I'm eager to bring my strings back to the rectory. I won't let Logan, or anything, frighten me away. With my favorite hat pulled to my ears, and my hair in a long, loose braid, I head out to compose.

The rectory is, as usual, dreary and shadowy. I set up in the farthest alcove — the one with the most light shining through. I tune up, and begin. The whole while, the vision of a ghostly boy in high boots and a billowy white shirt haunts my thoughts. My anger at him, and his bewildering anger at me, drive my bow faster.

Before I know it, dusk starts to creep in, and although the sun isn't out enough for there to be a sunset, the sky turns several amazing shades of purple. I stop playing and gaze up, my violin resting on my lap.

All at once, a cold sensation creeps over me, and a shiver shakes my body. I know — know — someone watches me. My heart pounds.

Not ten feet away, leaning against the stone wall of the rectory, with arms crossed over his chest, is Logan Munro. And he doesn't look so angry anymore.

This time, I don't blink. I don't scrub my eyes to make sure I'm not imagining things — I know I'm not. I simply keep my gaze on Logan.

He doesn't look away, either. He's illuminated enough so I can see the faultless cut of his jaw, his pale, smooth skin, and that dark wavy hair. I can barely draw a breath as Logan walks slowly in my direction.

"I guess you dunna frighten verra easy, Ivy Calhoun," he says.

I force myself to clear my throat. "Uh, no," I respond, surprised he knows my full name. I guess he's been hovering around, listening in. "I don't. Even when you try to choke me in the middle of the night."

Logan keeps his gaze locked on mine, frowning. "I did no such thing."

Now I'm confused. "You weren't in my room last night? Choking me until I couldn't breathe?"

His frown deepens. "Of course not. Why would I do that?"

"Because you want to scare me away. You want me gone. What did I ever do to you?"

Logan's eyes soften, and his intense gaze makes my insides seize. "'Tisna anythin' you did to me. Far from it." He shakes his head. "'Tis this place. Or somethin' that resides within. As I've said before, Glenmorrag's no' safe. There's somethin' here . . . unholy. I sense it. And it's gettin' stronger, if it was trying to harm you last night. 'Twas not me, lass. I swear it."

Logan has moved closer still. He now stands mere

inches away, and I can actually feel his energy taking up space. Somehow, I'm starting to believe him.

"Things have happened here in the past," he says quietly, his brow furrowing as if in deep thought. "Things that my memory won't recall. Just be careful, Ivy Calhoun."

The way he says my name, with that potent accent, leaves me breathless. I simply nod. "I always am, Logan Munro."

That brings a slow, delicious smile to his mouth, revealing straight white teeth. I stand from my seat in the alcove. It brings us closer in proximity than I predict.

Logan glances down at his booted feet, as if feeling shy. "'Tis a dangerous friendship to begin betwixt you and I, Ivy Calhoun. One that could be nothing more than heartache in the end. 'Tis how it is betwixt a human and a spirit."

That comment catches me totally off guard. While I'm thinking of how to respond, Logan asks, "Why do you play in here?"

"I . . . don't know. I guess I — it's beautiful, in its own desolate sort of way."

"Beautiful," Logan echoes, and his eyes linger over my face. I think my heart will slam right out of my chest. "Your music intrigues me," he adds. "You know, I am a musician myself." He reaches into his pocket and pulls out a small, slim flute.

"I know," I say. "I heard you playing. You play . . . very well."

Logan looks like he's almost blushing. It's hard to tell with a ghost, I guess. "My thanks," he says, dipping his head. "That means a great deal, coming from someone with your talent."

Now I'm the one who's blushing. I clear my throat, trying to take the focus off myself.

"I'm still going to find out how you died," I tell him, "and why you're still around."

"Aye?" he responds, raising one dark brow.

I clear my throat but maintain my gaze. "You can either help me or not. Either way, I'm doing it. It may even be tied to whatever else is going on around here. Got it?"

A slight smile touches his lips. "Persistent gell, aye?"

"Ivy? Who on earth are you talking to?"

I glance toward the entrance of the rectory to find Mom and Niall ducking inside. When I turn back to

Logan, he's gone. Or at least, invisible. I've no idea what his ghostly capabilities are. I find myself disappointed.

"No one, Mom," I lie, gathering my case and music folder and walking toward them. "I was . . . voicing my music. Remember?"

She laughs. "That's right. But it's getting dark out, sweetie. Come on, let's go eat."

As I walk through the decaying archway covered in ivy, I pause and glance over my shoulder. I don't see any handsome boys dressed in nineteenth-century clothing. But as I turn to follow Mom and Niall out, a voice — Logan's voice — whispers low in my ear.

"May I see you later?"

Chapter 8

I can't exactly tell Mom that I don't want to watch a DVD with her and Niall after supper because I have a date with a dead guy. That she and Niall actually want me to hang out with them is a miracle — or, guilt. Plus, Elizabeth is going to bed early, so I'd like to enjoy some time without her around.

Settling on the floor of the sitting room, at my mom's feet, I try not to act like I'm in a hurry to leave, but it's hard. Finally, the movie ends, and I wish her and Niall good night.

The moment I'm out of their sight I'm texting Emma, getting her up to speed on what's going on.

I want full details in the morn, luv, she texts back.

Absolutely.

As I hurry to the third floor, I'm suddenly unsure. Logan simply asked if he could see me later. Later could mean . . . much later. Couldn't it? Maybe I misinterpreted his request? Later in ghost lingo could really mean weeks, or months.

Oh, boy.

Just thinking about his request, spoken in his intriguing accent, gives me butterflies in my stomach. Why am I having such a reaction to him?

I open the door to my bedroom and he's there, leaning against my bedpost. It's clear he's been waiting. A slight grin lifts the corners of his mouth. My insides flutter. This is so much better than my clothes and violin floating through the air.

"So," I whisper, closing my door, "why did you stop trying to scare me?"

In the next instant, he's there beside me. Maybe two feet separate us. He looks so very real that it takes all of my strength not to try and touch him. Either the room is hot, or my body temperature is rising.

"Because I'm verra selfish," he answers quietly. He searches my face, slowly and meticulously. I find myself holding my breath, afraid of what he might think once he inspects me thoroughly. I've never given too much thought to my looks, but right now, I'm acutely aware of them.

His gaze returns to mine. "I suppose after all this time of watching you, I've grown to like you. No one's ever offered to help me before." He grins. "So I've appointed myself as your personal guardsman, since you willna leave, and since there's something else about." He pauses and looks at me expectantly. "If you'll have me?"

Wow. My own personal guardsman. And a cute one at that.

Back in Charleston, I had some crushes and went on a couple of dates with a couple of boys. I even was kissed — once. It was nothing special. Never, in the whole of my life, has a boy ever made me feel the way Logan does. I'm pretty positive it has a lot to do with the fact that he is from another century. Modern-day guys seem to lack something, and I guess I never realized that until now.

Corny as it sounds, it's chivalry.

"If you've given up trying to scare me into leaving Glenmorrag, then yes," I say. "I accept your offer." I sit on my window seat, pull my knees up, and lock them in place with my arms. "Can I ask you a question?"

His smile is mesmerizing. "Just one?"

A short laugh escapes my throat. "Not hardly. But I'll start out easy. How old are you?"

"Eighteen years."

My stare holds his. "So you were born in 1833, and you died —"

"One hundred and sixty-two years ago," he finishes. "I remember little of my life before my death. It's all very much a blur." His gaze clouds over, and we're quiet for a moment.

Boldly, I look right at him. "I . . . can't believe you're real."

His expression softens, and he gazes back intently. It almost makes me breathless.

"I thought the same thing of you," Logan says quietly, a muscle flexing in his jaw.

I know I blush clean to my roots. I shake my head, as if pretending what he said hasn't affected me as much as it has. By his expression, I know I've failed miserably on both accounts. I clear my throat. "So you can't remember anything at all? About the day you died? Is there anything . . . afterward, maybe?"

Logan studies the space of floor between his boots, deep in thought. "I have spots of memories, here and there," he says. He returns his gaze to mine. "I remember my mum. I remember hunting birds in the forests with my uncle. And I remember a powerful sense of danger. That might be my last real memory. And after you arrived here, that same sense of danger came rushing back to me. I immediately felt that something was amiss, and I feared for your safety."

"Well, after the freezer incident, and then the hands that were choking me, I fear for my safety, too," I say, hugging myself. "I thought it was you doing those things, but now I know it wasn't."

He nods, looking worried. "Aye. I did play those harmless pranks with your clothes and your violin. I also tried to simply tell you to leave. I thought those would suffice — that you might think there was a banshee present and you'd beg your mum to go. But I would never hurt you, Ivy."

"Thanks, Logan," I say, my face heating. I think I'll never tire of hearing him speak. His brogue fascinates me, and I hang on to every word. If he'd read a dictionary out loud, cover to cover, I'd be completely content. "So," I say, trying to focus back on all of the recent mysterious incidents, "do you think there's another spirit, then, out to get me?"

"It could very well be," Logan replies soberly. "There

are many who believe these old castles are thick with dark spirits who set out to harm newcomers in their midst."

"What about Elizabeth?" I ask, giving voice to my suspicions. "She really hates me. I don't know how she'd be making herself invisible, but . . ."

Logan furrows his brow. "Why do you feel Lady Elizabeth dislikes you so?"

"I can't decide if it's my pink hair" — I lift the streak to show him — "or the holes in my jeans."

"Have you no trousers to wear without holes?" he asks.

I laugh. "Of course. But it's the style now."

Logan grins. "Well, I fancy your hair. 'Tis unique."

I nod happily. "Thank you," I say, stifling a yawn.

"Och, you've school in the morn." He gives a low bow. "I'll be just outside your door, in my invisible state, of course, should you need anything." He smiles, wide and bright. "Good eve to you, Ivy. 'Till the morn."

"Good night," I whisper, feeling myself smile just as wide.

Logan promptly disappears, the whites of his teeth the last to go.

That night, I fall into a sounder, more restful sleep than I've had since I first arrived in Scotland.

Chapter 9

✎ MALEVOLENT ✎

When I wake up in the morning, I feel at ease knowing Logan's outside my door. I have some time before school, and I realize I'd like to see him again. I sit up in bed, smoothing out my hair and straightening out the long-sleeved music-camp shirt I sleep in. Then I call out to him.

He instantly appears, leaning against the bedpost. My heart speeds up at the sight of him.

"So, Logan Munro," I say, and settle back against my pillows, "when you're not guarding my door, what do you do here?"

Logan shrugs one shoulder. "I play my flute. I walk the lands. I visit the village. I do enjoy havin' a chat with

Ian, and Jonas. They both like to talk to me. Treat me as though I'm . . ." He sighs, then meets my gaze.

But I finish for him.

"Alive," I say.

Logan remains silent, but continues to watch me closely.

I shift forward, meeting his gaze. "You seem as real as anyone I know," I tell him.

Two short knocks against the door interrupt us, and then the door opens.

"Ivy?" my mother's voice calls out, just before her head pokes through the crack. "Ready for school?"

My gaze darts to first my mom, then Logan. He grins and places a single finger over his lips. Mom plops down on the bed, right where Logan stands at the foot. His grin widens just before he completely disappears. I fight the urge to smile back at him.

"Did you sleep well?" Mom asks, tightening the belt of her robe.

"I finally did," I say, slapping the fluffy mattress. "It's nice, Mom. All of it. Marriage. Niall. Scotland. Baby." I lean over and hug her. "And I'm glad you're so happy."

Mom's embrace tightens around me. "Oh, baby, thank you!" she says against my hair. Pulling back, she looks at me, and the hazy light casts her face in speckled dots of shadow. "I want you to be happy, too. The music you've come up with lately is amazing."

Pride squeezes my heart. It still feels good to get praise from my mom. "Thanks. I like it, too. I'm going to try out for the Strings of the Highlands concert coming up."

Mom grabs my hands. "You should do it, Ivy! You'll blow them away! Now come on, let's go downstairs," she says, standing up. "The staff is making a full Scottish breakfast and I'm dying for some spicy sausage."

My stomach growls at the mention of food. "Me too. Oh, I almost forgot. Can I have some friends over for Halloween? Just a few. You know, creepy castle and all. They think it'd be cool to hang out here."

Mom nods. "I think that'd be too fun. I'll get Niall to pick up some pumpkins to carve."

I laugh. "Great, Mom. I'll be down in a minute."

Mom waves as she slips out the door. For a few seconds, I stand and wait, fully expecting Logan to reappear. Instead, I only hear his voice.

"Your mum is wonderful," he says. "She has a lot of energy." He chuckles. "So, friends over for All Hallows' Eve, aye? Take care, Miss Calhoun. I shall see you later."

"See ya," I say back, and then I can sense that he's gone. It's strange but I sort of miss him already.

Breakfast is great — Elizabeth isn't present. After I eat, I hurry back upstairs to get my book bag.

On the second-floor landing, the air around me chills. I'm moving faster now, climbing the steps two at a time. The chill — it's weird. It's almost . . . chasing me. Nips at my calves, my elbows, and propels me forward until by the time I reach the third-floor landing, I'm at a dead run. Finally, I skid to a halt at my door, throw it open, leap inside, and slam the door shut behind me.

The dread clawing at me grabs my throat and squeezes. The chill seeps into the room and surrounds me, like icy fingers dragging across my skin. My breath puffs out in white drifts before me, fast, hard, and I watch it slip away to collect and hover in midair. It begins to form into a solid mass. The word *Die*.

I choke on my gasp. All at once the drawers on the armoire begin rattling. Soon, the rattle changes to slamming open and shut. The noise is deafening, and the armoire begins to rock back and forth. I cover my ears to drown out the noise.

"Logan," I say, almost in a whisper, my voice trembling, low. "Logan!"

He appears from thin air just as the armoire rocks one final time and slams toward me. I dive out of the way as it crashes to the floor.

"Cease!" Logan hollers.

At once, the room grows silent. The chill disperses, the horrible word in mist dissipates.

Logan's hands are balled into fists and his silver eyes are bright with anger.

"Are you hurt?" he asks. When I shake my head, he continues, his brows drawn in anger. "There is a malevolent presence here. I canna see it, but 'tis here all the same. This is no simple haunting. This is dark. I dunna want it coming anywhere close to you, Ivy."

"I don't know what I would've done if you weren't here," I say, feeling on the verge of tears. I look at him. "Thanks," I simply say, and it's not enough. I'm totally shaken up. How can I go to school after my life has been threatened like this?

All at once, my gaze lands on my bedside table.

No.

The photograph of my dad is gone. I drop to my knees to look beneath the table. I lift the bed skirt and peer into the shadows. Then I breathe a sigh of relief. It's there, facedown, in the center of the floor. I have to lie on my stomach and scoot partially underneath the bed to reach it. And that's not all I find.

Rising up, I lean back on my heels and glance up at Logan.

"How did this get under there?" I hold the other thing up. "What is this?"

Logan peers at the bundle of sticks in my hand. "Drop it, Ivy. Now!"

I let it go and it falls to the floor.

Logan sighs. "It's rowan. I'm willin' to bet it's cursed." He glances around the room and walks over to my poker. "Pick it up with your iron and throw it out the window." With a flick of his wrist, the window flies open.

Grabbing the fire poker, I lift the bundle of sticks, hurry over, and toss it out. I have no clue how the object got into my room, and it makes me shudder to think about someone sneaking in.

Then I turn to Logan, amazed.

"How is it you can open a window, or make my violin and clothes float in the air, but you can't make a poker hover?"

Logan shrugs. "Mostly, I can manipulate things that are light and porous. Those wooden frames in the window are of old wood. Your garments are light, too." He nods to the poker in my hand. "Solid iron? Nay." He nods again to the armoire. "And although that's wooden, it has iron pieces within. 'Tis too heavy."

I nod. "I didn't think about that."

"I'll let Jonas know about this" — Logan nods to the armoire again — "and we'll get it aright. I'll also search your room over for any more rowan." He looks at me. "Now, you go to school, and I'll be waiting for you when you get home. We'll figure out what to do next."

Chapter 10

✑ REMEMBRANCES ✑

At school, I grab Emma as soon as I find her and whisper to her what happened this morning. She looks appropriately horrified but wants to know more about Logan. Before I can elaborate, the prefect I met on my first day walks up to us.

"Ivy," Emma says, straightening up. "Remember I told you I'd introduce you to Serrus Munro again?"

Serrus flashes his bright smile. He really is handsome. "Hello again," he says.

"Hey," I say to him, feeling suddenly excited. Maybe he does know something about Logan. "So, is Munro an old name in the Highlands?" I ask. When a puzzled expression crosses his face, I quickly add, "I'm into genealogy."

"Aye," he says, nodding. " 'Tis an old name for sure. At least as far back as thirteen hundred or so." He inclines his head toward the forest edging the school's property. "About a half hour's drive that way I've an old tower house full o' Munro cousins."

"Yeah," Emma answers. "And one of them married a famous American fiction writer. Ethan and Amelia Munro. Right, Serrus?"

"Aye," he answers. "Amelia Landry-Munro. A fine lass. She writes about time travel and magic and such."

"And perfectly dreamy romance," Emma adds with a grin.

"Sounds like interesting reading." I'm thinking fast. If the Munro family goes back to the thirteen hundreds and they live in a castle hopefully filled with archives from their ancestors, chances are they could be Logan's kin.

"She wrote a bestseller, straight from the tower house," Serrus goes on.

"Oh, wow, that's cool," I admit. I love reading, and meeting a real live writer could be cool.

Serrus nods. "You're welcome tae come meet her if you'd like."

I blink.

"Of course she'd love to!" Emma says for me. "She's a bit shy. Unusual for an American, aye?" she laughs. "When?"

Serrus looks at Emma, then back to me. "Whenever she fancies."

The bell rings. "Thanks," I tell Serrus. "That would be great."

"Can I have your mobile number? I'll check to see when a good time for Amelia is, and I'll let you know." He throws a look at Emma. "You can come, too." He grins.

"Sweet," Emma says, whipping out her mobile. Her cheeks are a little flushed. Her fingers fly over the keyboard. "There. I just sent you Ivy's number." She smiles, very proud of herself.

As we part ways with Serrus and head to class, Emma grabs my elbow and whispers, "Going to the Munro home should be helpful, I hope."

I nod. "There's got to be something there. A ledger with family history in it? Something."

"Aye, probably so. We Scots fancy our history," Emma says. She pauses for a minute and then, looking impish, adds, "I've got tae meet him."

"Logan?" I whisper.

At that moment, we are joined by Derek and Cameron so we have to change the topic from ghosts to biology. Not nearly as fascinating.

When Mom and Niall pick me up after school, Mom looks excited. For the first time, too, she doesn't seem as pale and weak.

"Sweetie," Mom says as Niall drives toward the castle, "we're headed north up the coast to take a look at some more property Niall is interested in. Would you like to come?"

I don't hesitate. "Thanks, but I'll stay at the castle. Work on some new music." *And hang out with my new dead friend*, I think to myself.

So Mom and Niall drop me off at the castle. I hurry inside and up to my room to retrieve my violin. When I call softly for Logan, he appears.

"'Bout time you got home," he says. "It seems like it took forever."

This is, so to speak, music to my ears. "Want to go to the rectory?" I ask him. "I'm really wanting to compose."

He nods, and we head out of the castle together.

Outside it's silent, save for wind rustling the dying leaves and the noise my shoes make against the ground. Logan's boots make no sound at all.

"Tell me more about yourself, Logan," I say, and glance up at his face.

"I've wandered a lot," Logan says. A wave of dark hair falls across his alabaster forehead. "I'm no' bound to the castle, or even the lands," he continues. "Sometimes I find myself way up north, to the very tip of Scotland, and the time passes in a fashion I don't fancy. Once I wandered, and when I came back, three months had passed. It felt more like three days."

"It sounds lonely," I say as the rectory comes into view.

"It was," Logan says so quietly it's almost a whisper. "It has been, until now."

I've never been a big blusher, but I swear I can feel the heat move all the way up my throat to my face.

We enter the rectory, which is dim and shadowy, and both sit on a stone window seat. Logan sits bent over with his forearms resting against his knees, shoulders hunched.

"I wish I could recall how I came to be here, at Glenmorrag. All I know is, whatever happened to me was a long time ago."

I pull my legs up and wrap my arms around my knees. I like the way *ago* sounds like *agoo*.

Logan glances out one of the few remaining stained-glass windows. I have to keep myself from touching his face, or one of his hands. I follow his gaze, out of the once colorful glass embedded with the indigo head of a peacock. Although now faded and cracked, it stands stark against the cold gray stone. Somehow, it fits this place. So does Logan.

"But bad things have happened here, Ivy," he says, and looks directly at me. "I'm pretty sure I fell victim."

"Have you ever seen another spirit?" I ask.

He shakes his head. "Canna say that I have. And I've no' seen anything here. It's something that I feel. Whether 'tis a *taibhse* — ghostie — or a live being, I canna be sure. And that rowan under your bed? Someone put it there. Someone human." His gaze briefly moves in the direction of the castle before returning to mine. "Funny thing is, I didna feel the dark presence for a long, long time. Then, several years back, it returned."

I force myself to breathe. *Someone human.* "I keep thinking about Elizabeth," I admit.

Logan looks thoughtful. "She wasna always hateful. I

dunna recall all of her days here, but I do remember her as a playful, happy lass, laughing, running." He shrugs.

I try to picture a younger Elizabeth MacAllister, frolicking in the heather. I can't. The image just won't come.

I decide to turn our conversation toward the Munro clan.

"Don't you have any other family in Scotland?" I ask.

"If I do, lass, the ones who'd remember me are certainly all gone," Logan answers solemnly. "Why do you ask?"

"There's a boy named Munro at my school, and he has a bunch of Munro cousins. Might be worth checking out."

Logan nods. "It canna hurt."

"Oh," I say, something else occurring to me. "Would you consider . . . meeting someone?"

Logan looks at me with a glimmer in his silver eyes.

"A friend of mine. From school. Emma. She's the girl I brought here, to the rectory, last time. I trust her one hundred percent."

Logan's gaze locks onto mine. "Aye. If you trust her, then I will as well."

Before I can stop myself, my hand reaches toward his arm. "Thanks —"

And it slips right through him.

"Oh, shoot," I say, and jerk my hand back. "Sorry about that."

The glimmer in Logan's eyes brightens. "It's all right," he says, his raspy voice quiet. "Doesna bother me." Then he inclines his head toward my violin. "Will you play now?"

Settling my violin against my chin, I pull the bow across the strings and start the new melody. It comes easy.

And while I play, the ghost of a murdered boy watches me. When did my life become so crazy?

Chapter 11

✑ THE MUNROS ✑

*H*ome from school the next day, I dash up the stairs. Logan is waiting at the second-floor landing.

"Hey," I say, grinning.

"Hey yourself," he responds, mimicking my Charleston drawl.

"Very funny," I comment as we walk to my room. "I spoke to the headmistress today about the Strings festival entry and I filled out forms, so I'm all set. She wants to hear the piece I'm working on."

"No doubt she'll fancy it."

I give him a smile. "Thanks."

My heart skips a beat as we stand there, eyes locked.

"Okay," I say, and I notice how the grin on Logan's mouth spreads. "Well, let me change out of my monkey suit." I glance down at my school uniform. I had worn the black pants today.

Logan chuckles. "I'll be right here," he answers, and leans against the doorjamb. "Although I'd fancy seeing a monkey in a suit."

Shaking my head, I shut the door. Just as I cross the room to my armoire, my cell phone vibrates. A text message. It's Serrus.

If you're up to it, come to the Munro Tower House today. My cousin Ethan's wife Amelia will be around. 4pm? I've already texted Emma and she can come.

Excitedly, I respond.

Totally up for it. Thanks!

I start to think about what I want to ask the Munros. *Change clothes, Ivy*, I remind myself. Once I do, I call to Logan.

"Aye?" he asks as he appears.

As I power up my laptop, I answer. "That Munro I met at school? He just invited me and Emma to come over and meet his cousins." As I talk, I Google Amelia Landry. Several pages appear, and I choose one that's an interview with a local paper.

"What are you doing?" Logan asks.

"I'm looking them up online," I answer. "Munro's wife is a famous author." I grin. "I want to be prepared when I meet them."

"I have seen this strange machine of yours before," he says, leaning over my shoulder and staring at the screen. "I dunna think I can decipher all the words. My mum had started teaching me how to read, you know. Before."

I look at Logan. "I'll pick up where she left off, if you like," I offer. He smiles and nods, and I read out loud from the *Highlands Gazette*. "'Amelia Landry-Munro is a bestselling American author of multiple works of fiction. She is married to Laird Ethan Arimus Munro of the Munro clan in the Highlands of Scotland.'"

Amelia's website is listed, and I click the link. It's a beautifully designed site, with lots of scrollwork and castle art. There's a picture of her most recent book, called *Enchanted Love*. I read the book's description aloud.

"'An American girl deep in the Scottish Highlands stumbles upon an enchanted tower house and its enchanted inhabitants, in the form of fourteenth-century Scottish warriors. She fights to help end the curse that has bound them as spirits for hundreds of years — and to keep her heart intact as she falls in love with one of them, a fierce knight.'"

An American girl in the Scottish Highlands? Spirits? This story hits a bit too close to home.

"I've gotta get that book," I say, and glance at Logan. He raises one dark eyebrow and grins.

"Fanciful stories of love and enchanted knights? I'm no' too sure that will help solve the mystery o' my death."

I laugh and continue checking out the website. "You never know, Mr. Doubtful." I click on Amelia's photo gallery. Several selections show her at book signings and conferences. "Wow," I say. "She's really pretty."

"Aye," Logan answers, peering closely.

I'd elbow him, if I could.

Then I see a photo of Amelia and a huge guy. His arm is wrapped protectively around her shoulders. The caption reads *Amelia, with her laird husband, Ethan Munro.* They're standing in front of an enormous tower castle.

I gasp as I get a good look at the laird.

"No way," I mutter just as Logan mutters, "Och, damn."

Laird Ethan Munro has dark hair, light skin, a square-cut chin, and very unusual pewter-colored eyes. . . .

Though he's older than Logan, the resemblance is

uncanny. Logan and I stare at each other, silent for several seconds.

"You look just like him," I finally say. "It's . . . weird how much you look alike."

"Aye," he answers. "Mayhap we're kin after all?"

I scroll through the rest of Amelia's picture gallery. One photo in particular stands out — it's Ethan and his kinsmen. Six men in all.

"They're . . . so huge. Like, linebacker huge," I say.

"What's linebacker?" Logan asks.

I chuckle. "Football guys. Not soccer. American football." I shake my head. "I'll tell you all about it later." I study the Munros. "There's something just not . . . right about them." I shake my head and peer closer. "Something different. I can't put a finger on it."

"Like what?" Logan asks, staring at the photo.

I shrug, reading their names in the caption. *Ethan, Rob, Gilchrist, Torloch, Aiden, Sorely.* A lot of the names sound very old-fashioned.

Then I notice the time in the right-hand corner of the screen. "I should go," I say, grabbing my coat. "I'm going to ask Jonas if he'll drive me over." I open the door, then spin back around toward Logan. "Are you coming?"

Logan presses his hand over his heart. "You wound me to think otherwise."

As I step out into the hall, I almost plow over Trudy, the young maid, carrying a load of clean towels. She glances behind me, then behind herself.

"Are you speakin' tae me, then?" she asks.

I'm not very good at lying, so my cover-up is awkward. "Oh, are those for my bathroom?" I ask, pointing at the towels. "I'll take them in if you like."

Trudy doesn't look like she's buying it. "Eh, no," she says. She stares at me as though I have a horn growing in the middle of my forehead. "That's okay, gell. 'Tis my job."

"Well, thanks," I say, continuing as though nothing is wrong. But Trudy's eyes remain on me until I disappear from sight.

"I'm no' sure she believes you, Ivy," Logan says. "You're a terrible liar."

Pinching the metal tab on my down coat between my fingers, I yank the zipper all the way up. "Tell me about it. It's why I hardly ever even try. Let's find Jonas."

He's easy to find. In the kitchen, going over menus.

"Hey, Jonas," I say. "Do you think you could drive me somewhere?"

"Sure, Miss Ivy, where to?"

"To the Munro Tower House."

"I'll take her, Jonas," Niall cuts in, strolling into the kitchen. He and Mom are heading off on another drive today, to see yet another property. "Her mother and I are aimed in that direction anyway."

I turn to my stepfather. "Thanks, Niall. I didn't want to bother you."

"No bother, Ivy. Are you ready to go now?" he asks.

"I am, yes," I answer.

Niall turns when my mom walks in. "Love, we're going to drop Ivy off at the Munros'."

Mom breaks out into a smile. "More new friends, Ivy? That's wonderful!"

I wonder if she'd feel differently knowing that these friends might be relatives of a ghost.

We all head outside and climb into the Rover. Logan materializes beside me in the backseat, and I try hard not to look at him and smile. But the moment the car starts moving, Logan disappears. One second he's there, the next, gone. Turning my head, I glance around, and through the back window I see him, standing in the drive.

What the heck? Why did he get out? I almost want to tell Niall to stop the car so I can jump out and run back to Logan, but I know he and Mom would be concerned for my mental health. So I sigh and try not to worry about Logan.

Instead, I pull up Serrus's latest text on my phone. I tell Niall, "Here's the address —"

"Och, no need, Ivy. I know the Munro house," Niall says. "We'll be there in no time. Now, what is it that interests you there?"

"Well," I say, and I hardly know what *else* to say. "One of the kids at school is a Munro," I answer. "I thought it was kinda cool that his cousin is an American author. So he asked if I wanted to meet her."

"Right. Ethan Munro's wife. Nice lass," Niall says. He glances at Mom. "I meant to tell you, Julia — Lady Amelia is from Charleston, too."

"Oh, how interesting," Mom says. "Ivy, do you know of her?"

"Not until now," I reply. I glance out the window, and over my shoulder, but there's no sign of Logan. Where is he?

Finally, a little more than thirty minutes east, in the dead center of the Highlands, we come to the long drive leading to the Munro Tower House. Ancient stone, gray and blackened with time, rises from the mist sliding across the ground. It looks even older than Glenmorrag, and even spookier, if that's possible.

Niall pulls around a gravel drive and stops at the front steps. Serrus and Emma are already there, waiting outside the front doors. Emma comes straight over. She's looking in the Rover, and all around. I know she's searching for Logan. We all get out and I introduce Serrus to Niall and Mom.

"How ya doin', Yank?" Serrus says to me.

I give him a grin. "Same ole, same ole," I answer, and he chuckles.

That's when the massive, double-hung oak doors swing open and the six giant men I recognize from the photos online step out into the fading dusk. They stand in a huddle, arms crossed over bulky chests, legs braced to support their weight.

"Looks like Munro could have his own rugby team," Niall says with an impressed laugh. "Big lads."

"They are indeed," Serrus says proudly.

And they really, really are. I immediately pick out Ethan Munro.

He looks even more like a grown-up version of Logan in person. A lump forms in my throat, and I swallow past it. I have to make myself not stare at him.

"Och, MacAllister," Ethan says, stepping forward and extending a hand. "Good of you tae visit." He glances toward Serrus. "I see you've met my wee cousin."

"Aye," Niall says, shaking Ethan's hand.

Ethan nods toward the other men. "My brothers, Rob and Gilchrist, and cousins Aiden, Sorely, and Torloch."

The men all give a nod.

Niall drapes his arm around Mom's shoulder. "Munro, this is my bride, Julia. I told you about her, as you recall?"

Ethan lifts Mom's hand and kisses the top of it. "Pleasure, Lady MacAllister. Welcome tae Scotia."

I watch as red stains my mom's cheeks. It's almost funny.

Until the laird turns his attention to me. Not so funny anymore.

Ethan Munro's mercury gaze lights on mine, and I fight the urge to look away. He towers over me. "You must be Ivy. Serrus has told me about you." He extends that huge paw of a hand to me, and I take it in as firm a shake as I can muster.

"Yes, sir," I answer.

"Ah," Ethan says, his eyes softening. "You've the accent of my beloved bride, Amelia. You hail from Charles Town, yes?"

I smile and glance at Mom. Charles Town is the old name of my home city. "All my life, until now," I answer.

"MacAllister, you and your lady will stay and visit for a while?" Ethan asks.

"Och, this time, nay," Niall answers. "We're on our way to oversee a pub I have the mind tae buy. Next time, mayhap?"

"Aye," Ethan says. "Good trip to you, then."

"Cheers," Niall says to Ethan. "We'll pick you up on our way home, Ivy," he says.

I thank him, then kiss Mom good-bye, and watch them get back into the Rover.

"Let's go inside, then," Ethan says.

We all file in. Emma crams against my side.

"Where is he?" she whispers in my ear.

"Still back at the castle, I think," I whisper back, and Emma frowns. "Don't worry," I assure her. "He wants to meet you, too. Halloween probably."

Every one of Emma's teeth shows as she grins.

"Sae, cousin," Ethan says. "I see you've swayed another lass tae tolerate your company, as well."

"Aye, so it seems," Serrus responds with a chuckle. "This is Emma."

Ethan shakes her hand, too, and she looks at me and mouths, *He is so hot.*

I hide a smile with my hand. Emma is so crazy.

Ethan leads us to the great hall. A large fireplace occupies one wall, and the blaze snaps and sizzles. There are two leather sofas, several chairs, and recliners, too.

"Take a seat, Ivy, Emma," Ethan suggests. "Amelia is finishing something in her office. She'll join us shortly."

Emma and I sit in two old-looking chairs, covered in mossy-green velvet. Serrus plops onto the arm of Emma's chair.

"Sae, how are you finding our country?" Ethan says, sitting across from us. The other men find various places to perch, listening closely. The room seems to grow smaller with all those Munros in it.

I take a deep breath. "Fascinating. I've gotten very interested in the history and people of the region. I was even wondering if you knew enough of your family history to trace back to one . . . person in particular."

Ethan and the others stare at me, waiting.

"A boy," I continue.

One of Ethan's eyebrows lifts, along with the corner of his mouth. *So much like Logan . . .*

I try to gather a little more courage. "His name is Logan Munro. He was born in 1833 and died when he was eighteen." I meet Ethan's gaze. "I . . . think he was murdered."

Ethan strokes his chin. "And where do you get such information, lass?" he inquires.

Silently, I stare at him, refusing to tell him the truth. I *can't*. He'll think I'm insane. Or will he? "I've just . . . heard, is all. Rumors from the staff at the castle. I'd like to find out, if I can."

Ethan leans forward, his elbows on his knees. "Many a Munro has died a dreadful death over the centuries, lass. Early Scotia was a vicious land." He rubs his chin. "There once was a lad named Jaime. He had sons — several o' them. They had sons, and so on. By the by, a bonny lass named Mirrah was born. She bore a son. He was Logan."

I blink, stunned.

"Looked enough like me to be my twin, at that age."

I cock my head at his comment.

"Or so I've heard," Ethan adds, clearing his voice. "'Tis a shame, though. The boy was thought to have died, possibly by murder. His body was never found."

"Ethan Arimus Munro," a woman's voice — with an accent just like mine — breaks the air. "Shame on you."

The guys all erupt in chuckles.

"Och, wife," Ethan says. "I'm no' doin' a thing wrong. Just tellin' the lass here about a relative."

"Well, I thought she came to see a fellow Charlestonian." A tall, willowy blonde woman enters the room and walks up to Ethan.

"Ivy, I'm Amelia." She smiles and inclines her head. She has almond-shaped blue-green eyes. "This lunkhead's wife. Come on," she says, and motions to me and Emma. "Let's leave this chamber of testosterone, girls. I've something to show you."

I press my lips together to keep from laughing out loud. "Sounds good to me," I answer. Emma and I hastily trail behind Amelia.

She leads us through the tower house and up a set of spiral steps leading to an enormous library. Lining the walls are portraits of people from long ago.

"Impressive, aren't they?" Amelia says. "Ethan's younger brother, Gilchrist, painted them all. From memory."

"That's amazing," I say. Meanwhile, I think, *From memory? Did Gilchrist* know *these clearly long-dead people?* The portraits look so real, and detailed.

Amelia then heads straight to a particular shelf and retrieves an old ledger. She moves to a desk and inclines her head for us to join her. Amelia opens the book and begins searching the pages.

"I heard you telling Ethan you're interested in the family tree. This is our Munro clan history," she says. "We're not the only Munros in Scotia, so says my husband. Here." She flips the book around in my direction and points to a section marked *1800–1900.* "Just as Ethan says, a boy was born to a Mirrah Munro, and disappeared without a trace eighteen years later." She turns the book back and reads on. "Seems there was an uncle, Patrick Munro, who died a few weeks later. Mirrah's brother." She shakes her head. "His body was found at the base of the cliffs." She raises her gaze. "At Glenmorrag Castle. It says he and his nephew had been hired as musicians for the laird and lady at the time."

My heart's beating a mile a minute as I stare at the written names and dates. This has to be some sort of clue. Was Logan's death somehow linked to his uncle's?

"That's amazing, to have so much family history written in one book," I say, and read on. "Wow. It says Logan's mother died of natural causes at the ripe old age of eighty-three."

Amelia points to one of the portraits on the wall. "We don't have a portrait of Logan, unfortunately. But this one here is Patrick. And here . . ." She points to another one. "This is Mirrah. Very young, of course."

I stare in disbelief. *I'm looking at Logan's mother,* I say to myself. She's beautiful, with long, dark curls and full lips. My gaze then moves to Mirrah's brother, Logan's uncle. Patrick. A handsome guy, with physical traits just like the other Munros.

As I stare at him, something strikes me as . . . familiar. I can't put a finger on it.

"Lady Munro, may I use the loo?" Emma asks.

"Sure, sweetie," Amelia says. "There's one just up the hall."

"Thanks," Emma says, and grins at me. "Be right back." She slips out the door.

"Ivy," Amelia says after Emma leaves. I look at her, and her eyes are searching mine. "Do you notice anything . . . different about my husband and his kinsmen?"

I nod.

Amelia smiles. "Can you tell me what?"

I think about it. "It's their speech. Their mannerisms. They don't seem . . . modern. I guess." I kind of laugh. "Like they're extras that stepped out of the movie *Braveheart*."

Her smile widens. "Let me fetch you another book." She stands and heads to a different section of the library. I see an impressive row of books all with Amelia's name on the spine. She plucks one such book off the shelf and brings it over to me.

"I know Serrus told you I'm an author," she says with a modest smile. "Now, this may not be exactly your taste, but I think you might find this interesting. Try to read it with an open mind. And when you're finished, we'll talk again."

The book is a copy of *Enchanted Love*. My eyes rise to meet hers.

"I was going to order a copy anyway," I tell her, excited. "It sounds fantastic."

Her gaze continues to search mine. "Have you seen Logan Munro?"

I almost jerk back at her blunt question. "I, um," I stutter.

Amelia smiles and holds up her hand. "It's okay. Seriously. Read the book. Then give me a call." She jots her telephone number down on a piece of paper and hands it to me.

"I . . . don't understand," I say. I want to tell her, and Ethan, *Yes! Your cousin is haunting my castle!* but I just can't. I'm not sure what stops me. Maybe it's because I really don't know Amelia. She seems nice and trustworthy, though.

"What'd I miss?" Emma says, walking back into the library.

Amelia grabs another copy of *Enchanted Love* and hands it to her. "In case you'd like to read it, too."

"Och, thanks," Emma says, and stares at the cover. "Brilliant."

"You're welcome. Now, we best head back into the great hall before the laird comes looking for us," Amelia says.

As we leave, I glance at the portraits once more. Patrick Munro stands tall, with his foot braced against a large rock.

He's wearing dark brown pants, leather boots, a white long-sleeved shirt, and a vest. His hand is resting on his bent knee. Long mahogany hair flows over his shoulders. I study the portrait some more, and there's still something that bugs me about it, but I can't place what it is.

We find Ethan and the others, and get ready to leave. As I pass Aiden, he gives me a grin. "Be seein' you 'round, lass," he says quietly. I'm not really sure what to think of it, so I say nothing in return. It's like they all know something. A secret. One that they enjoy keeping.

"Och, you each have a copy of the book," Serrus says, inclining his head to the novel tucked under my arm. "Amelia's great, aye?"

"Flattery will get you everywhere, darling," Amelia says, giving Serrus a hug. "This one here reads all of my work," she says. The other Munros all chuckle.

Serrus's cheeks turn red, and I notice him shoot a glance at Emma. I'm starting to suspect he likes her, and that my friend might share his affections.

"Och, leave the lad be," Ethan says, and gives Serrus a gentle shove. "Dunna be a stranger 'round here, cousin."

Serrus shakes his hand. "I willna. And thanks for having us over."

"Yes," I say. "Thank you." I look at Amelia and smile.

Amelia puts her hand up to her ear like a phone. *Call me*, she mouths.

My phone vibrates then, and it's a text from Mom. They're pulling into the Munro drive. Just in time. I follow Serrus and Emma out the door.

Niall and Mom pull up, and I get inside the Rover, my thoughts tumbling. Emma climbs on the back of Serrus's motorcycle, and they wave to me. I can't help but think they make a cute couple.

"What do you have there?" Niall asks after we're down the driveway.

"Lady Munro gave me a copy of her book," I answer, and already I know it's way more than just a simple novel. "I'm going to start reading it tonight."

Chapter 12

ALL HALLOWS' EVE

"*W*hat happened to you?" I ask Logan the second I see him outside my room in Glenmorrag. "Where'd you go?"

"I dunno," he answers. "Once the laird's Rover started to move, I . . . shifted out of it."

"Maybe it has to do with physics and space and time," I say, opening the door to my room. I'm not scared to enter anymore now that Logan has been standing guard. "Your intangible self can't keep up with a moving vehicle. I don't know, I'm guessing. What is so funny?"

"You missed me," he says matter-of-factly, grinning. "Did you no'?"

I slip him a sideways glance. "Dunna be so cocky, boy," I say.

Logan's laugh is deep and resounding. "That's a very nice brogue you have there, Ivy."

I'm eager to tell Logan about my visit to the Munros. I set my copy of *Enchanted Love* on the writing desk, and then Logan and I sit side by side on my window seat.

"I found out some very interesting stuff at the Munros," I tell him. I take a deep breath. "The Munros are your relatives, Logan. Cousins. Your name was in their family ledger. I saw a portrait of your mother, Mirrah. And of your uncle Patrick. He died a few weeks after you went missing, according to the family history. He was employed here at the castle, along with you. He died here."

Logan's eyes widen. "Wha — how?"

"I guess an accident. His body was found at the base of the sea cliffs out back."

"Saint's blood," he whispers.

I nod. "The ledger also says," I add, a little quieter, "that you disappeared and were never found."

"Aye," he answers. Rubbing his jaw, he looks at me. "Anything about my mother?"

I smile. "She lived to be eighty-three."

A broad smile breaks his handsome face in two. "You did a fine job, gell," he says. "I thank you for it. And to think . . ." He shakes his head. "I've family no' too far from here. All this time, and I never knew."

"Or, you just didn't remember," I offer. "Now you know, though. You can visit."

" 'Twouldna do a bit of good if they dunna believe in the unliving," he says. "In me."

"I don't know why, Logan, but my gut tells me these Munros will believe. And if you have to remain here, on this — you know, this plane or whatever," I continue, "then at least you can have a family again."

Suddenly, the thought of not having Logan around really bothers me.

"Aye," he agrees. "There is that."

"Do you think your uncle Patrick's spirit is here?" I ask.

Logan thinks a moment. "If it was, why wouldna he be in the same form as myself? Nay," he decides. "I dunna think so, Ivy." He looks at me. "We'll figure it all out."

"We will," I agree. I glance at the digital clock on my nightstand. "I'd better get ready for bed. Not only is it school tomorrow, but it's Halloween."

A slow smile tips the corners of Logan's mouth. "Aye, so it is. What sort of plans do you have cookin' in that head of yours?"

"I don't know. Emma's coming over. If she doesn't meet you soon, I think she'll self-combust. And the MacLeod twins are coming, too. Not sure if they'll believe, but they're cool." Logan's stare is making me blush again. "I think we're going to carve pumpkins and tell spooky stories or something."

"Well," he says, and stands. Shoving his hands into his pockets, he grins. "What better way to have a spooky All Hallows' Eve than to have a real spirit tell the tale, aye?"

I grin. "We'll see about that. Have a good night, Logan."

With a low bow, Logan smiles. "I'll be just out the door if you need me."

I blink, and he's gone.

Quickly, I change into some warm sweatpants and a thermal top, grab my copy of *Enchanted Love*, and climb beneath the covers. Flipping past the first few pages, I read the dedication.

For my very own enchanted knight, Ethan. And to your kinsmen. By the by . . .

Interesting. Then I begin to read. Very quickly, I get completely lost in the story.

Enchanted Love seems to have a lot of similarities to reality. It's the story of an American author with writer's block who goes to stay in a supposedly haunted Scottish tower house for inspiration. What she finds there is a group of handsome guys led by their clan leader, whom the American falls in love with. The men have been enchanted for centuries. They walk as spirits during the day, but during the gloaming hour — that space of time between dusk and darkness — they gain substance and are mortal. The whole while I'm reading, I see Amelia as the heroine, and Ethan as the hero. It seems so . . . real. Fantastically so.

I read and read until my eyes can't stay open anymore. Finally, I drift off with the book still in my hands.

When I wake up, it's six A.M. I've only slept for four hours. With a groan, I climb out of bed, grab my clean uniform for the day, and slip out the door to go shower. Logan is sitting in the corridor, back against the wall, knees pulled up. His arms are resting atop them. Our eyes meet, and he leaps to his feet.

"You're up early," he says, grinning.

"I didn't go to sleep until two," I yawn, and start toward the bathroom. "I was so into Amelia's book."

"Och, girl, you'll be sorry you did that about midday," he jokes.

"I know," I sigh.

I shower quickly and am just stepping out of the tub, wrapped in a large white towel, when I hear a dull thud come from the small window by the sink.

I jump in reaction to the noise, but when I glance at the window, nothing is there.

I shrug. With the heel of my palm, I wipe the moisture from the mirror and peer at my image. Straight, sopping-wet blonde hair. Pale skin. Wide, light eyes. Nothing special or exotic. But I wonder what Logan thinks when he looks at me. I smile.

Thud.

This time, the noise is louder, sharper, and I scoot backward to glance up. A large black shape fills the window.

Thud! Thud thud thud thud thud!

A gasp escapes my throat. Over and over the dark shape smashes against the pane of glass until it breaks through. As the black object hurls across the bathroom, I let out a scream.

It hits the wall and falls to the floor.

Logan materializes beside me.

"Ivy!" he says, inching closer, hand out to calm me. "What's the matter, lass?"

Wet hair falls in my face, and I push it back. The object on the floor is still moving.

"There," I say, pointing.

"Och," Logan says. "'Tis a raven."

My heart is beating like crazy in my chest, but I crouch beside the raven. In its mouth is a small piece of bark, or maybe a torn branch. "Shh," I croon to the injured bird. Slowly, I reach out and remove the twig. The inky bird stares at me with its yellow eye, and I try stroking its head with my finger.

Then the raven instantly squawks, hops up, and flies out the broken window.

"Whoa!" I say, reeling back.

"Are you all right?" Logan asks, looking over at me. I'm suddenly aware I'm still in just a towel.

"I'm fine!" I announce, my skin flushing. "I'm not dressed —"

"I can see that, lass," he says, grinning.

"Out!" I demand, but can't help but smile back.

The moment he disappears, I set the twig on the counter, dry off as fast as I can, and put on my uniform, confused and terrified by my encounter with the raven.

In the corridor, Logan awaits me.

"What was in its mouth?" he asks.

I hold out the twig. "I don't know. It looks like a piece of a tree."

Logan nods. "Rowan. 'Tis the same as that bundle you found under your bed, remember? 'Tis cursed, Ivy. Put it down."

"Oh," I answer, and set it on a hall table. I stare at the dark brown woody scrap. "That's just . . . great."

Logan frowns. "What are the chances of a raven picking up a rowan twig and bashing through your window just to give it to you?" He shakes his head. "I dunna like this."

I shiver. Neither do I. "It's so weird that as soon as I took the twig, the raven flew away. It's almost as if it came specifically for me. Like someone was controlling it."

Logan nods. "Aye. Like a live spell."

"Perfect way to start Halloween off, huh?" I say.

Logan's expression grows serious. "Be careful today. All Hallows' Eve is more than just dressing up and pinching sweets. 'Tis Samhain. At the bewitching hour, the bridge between the living and the dead closes. 'Tis a gap easily gained by either."

I can't help but shiver again.

Outside the school, Emma is pacing at the drop-off line, waiting for me. I'm glad to see her — it takes my mind off the crazy raven incident.

"So," Emma says as we weave through the kids flocking to class, "I brought clothes to change into for later. Are you sure your mum doesna mind the lot of us coming over tonight?"

"Nope, not at all. My mother loves Halloween as much as she loves Christmas. I have a feeling by the time we get to the castle she'll have black paper bats hanging through the great hall."

"I'd like to see her get that past old Lady MacAllister," Emma laughs, and I groan. I've been trying not to think about Elizabeth too much lately.

The day passes quickly. Though there are no paper bats and jack-o'-lanterns in the classrooms, there's a definite feel of Halloween in the air. The misty wind outside adds to the spookiness. I get a twinge of excitement, along with a ping of dread.

After school, I can tell Emma is very eager to meet Logan, though she keeps quiet about it in the car with my mom and Niall. The Rover is barely at a full stop when Emma leaps from the car, pulling me along with her.

"Thanks for letting me come over," Emma calls to Mom and Niall.

"Anytime, sweetie," Mom replies. "Burgers and fries tonight, girls! A real American meal. And Niall is heading off now to get the pumpkins."

"Brilliant!" Emma says, and together we go through the door and head up the stairs. Emma is two steps ahead of me. Nearly dragging me.

"Okay, okay!" I say, laughing. "Hold your horses."

All of a sudden I slam straight into Emma's back. If she didn't have the death grip on my arm, I would stumble right back down.

"Em, watch it —"

Steadying myself, I move next to her and look straight ahead. Logan is there, shoulder against the wall, one booted foot crossed over the other.

I all but lose my breath.

He is *so* handsome.

"Logan," I say, and look at Emma, whose eyes are as round as saucers. "This is my friend Emma. Who obviously totally believes in spirits. Emma, Logan."

Logan gives Emma a slight nod. "My pleasure."

Emma blinks. And says nothing.

"Emma!" I say.

"Right," she says, finding her voice. "Hiya."

I laugh. "Wow, something to hold Emma's tongue. It's a miracle."

Emma doesn't take her eyes off Logan, even as he falls into pace with us in the hallway. I lead us into my room, but I halt Logan.

"We'll change, and then go out to the rectory," I say with a grin. "Wait right here."

Logan's eyes are piercing. "I'm glad you're home. 'Tis a long day whilst you're gone."

My heart skips as I shut the door.

Emma immediately grabs me. "You didna tell me he was gorgeous!"

"He's a ghost," I say. "But he can still hear you."

A chuckle comes from the other side of the door.

Emma gives me a long look.

I frown. "What?"

"You fancy him," she whispers. "Dunna ya?"

The chuckles from the doorway stop.

I bite my lip.

"I can see it in your eyes," she continues.

"Emma," I start warningly, but lucky for her, her cell phone buzzes. She reaches into her pocket and from her smile and blush, I can tell it's Serrus. She tells me he's coming over later, too, and now it's my turn to tease her a little. "Look who's blushing now," I say. Emma just grins.

We change quickly — I put on distressed jeans and an orange-and-black long-sleeved button-down shirt. Emma wears a pair of jeans, and an orange shirt that has a black cat wearing a striped, pointy witch's hat on it.

"Cute," I say, grabbing my violin and bow. Together, we head out.

Logan is waiting in the corridor. He focuses on me, and Emma focuses on him.

"The twins and Serrus won't be here for a couple of hours," I say. "Wanna go to the rectory?"

"Will you play some?" Logan asks.

"Sure," I answer, and suppress a giggle as I notice Emma still staring.

"I'll meet you both there," Logan says, and vanishes. Emma gasps out loud at the sight. I don't think her mouth closes fully until we're outside the castle doors.

The wind is sharp and chilly, and it leaves a barren feeling in its wake. Emma and I make our way to the rectory and duck through the broken archway.

"Where is he?" Emma says, glancing around.

"You girls move fast," Logan says, materializing from the shadows.

Emma squelches a holler.

"Logan," I scold. "She's not used to you yet."

He gives Emma a quick grin. "Sorry 'bout that."

"Right, no problem, then," Emma says, and eases onto the stone seat by the window.

"It's nice finally tae meet you," Logan says to Emma. "Ivy has told me all about you."

Emma relaxes the more they chat, and soon she's ninety to nothing, asking Logan every question under the moon. I think I prefer the silent, cat-has-her-tongue Emma over this one.

But while they talk, Logan keeps meeting my gaze, and giving me small smiles.

"Are you sure you're ready to meet one of your cousins?" I ask him.

Logan nods. "Aye, more than ready," he says, then frowns. "What if he doesna believe?"

"I know. I'll keep the twins busy outside while you introduce Logan to Serrus," Emma tells me. "We'll see how it goes."

And that's exactly what we do. Serrus arrives just a few minutes ahead of the twins, whose mom drops them off at the front of the castle. While Emma distracts them by pointing out the peacocks, Serrus comes to the rectory. I meet him at the archway.

"Remember that boy I was asking your cousin Ethan about?" I whisper to him.

Serrus nods. "Aye, indeed. Logan."

I glance over my shoulder. "Logan?" I call.

Serrus's silver eyes, so much like Ethan's and Logan's, are questioning.

Then they widen as Logan materializes before us.

"Cousin," Logan offers first.

Serrus lets out a sigh, then glances at me. "Ivy! I dunna believe it. You coulda told me a while back." He grins at

Logan. "Och, but you look just like our other cousin, Ethan."

Logan nods. "Aye, Ivy here showed me his image on her computer screen."

Serrus runs his hand through his hair. "So. We've much to discuss, aye?"

Logan nods. "Aye, indeed."

As far as ghosts meeting mortals go, I'd say this one went pretty well.

I'm about to ask Serrus more questions about the Munros when Emma texts me. Apparently my mother and Niall are calling us inside for dinner, and the twins are threatening to eat all the food in the castle. I bid Logan a quick good-bye before Serrus and I head off. Logan promises me he won't stray far from my side tonight.

Elizabeth is resting up in her room tonight, so dinner is a fun, informal affair: hamburgers with the works, French fries, and black-and-orange frosted cupcakes, courtesy of Mom, for dessert. When we're done, Derek, Cam, Emma, Serrus, and I set up out back, near the hedge maze, and carve the pumpkins Niall brought from the market. Mom brings us candles, and when we're finished, we light up the jack-o'-lanterns and set them on the stone wall. It makes for a perfectly eerie Halloween sight. I'd be having a blast if the incident with the raven, and Logan's earlier warning, weren't echoing in my head.

Logan keeps to his promise, though, and hovers off to the side all night. He smiles at me when I glance his way. I'm glad it's dark outside because I can feel the heat stain my cheeks.

"How 'bout a run through the maze?" Serrus challenges.

"Ivy, you don't count 'cause you live here," Derek says with a grin. "You probably already know the route."

"I have no clue what the route is," I say truthfully. "But I'm up for it if the rest of you are."

"Let's split into groups," Derek suggests, linking his arm through his sister's. "Cam and I will go with Ivy."

Emma and Serrus exchange a shy glance. "I guess we'll go together," Emma says, and Serrus beams.

Set in our groups, we all take off.

Only the light from a three-quarter moon spills over the hedges and into the maze. Shadows lean awkwardly, and more times than once, I'm fooled by the illumination. I'm comforted knowing Logan is close by, watching.

When one of those crazy peacocks screams out, Cam echoes with a scream of her own. Laughter erupts through the maze.

It's almost tempting to forget the frightening things going on at the castle and to just enjoy Halloween with new friends. No such luck. Suddenly, the mist grows thicker, edging its way between me and the twins up ahead. Clouds move in front of the moon. I hurry along the path, until I bump into the hedge. Backing up, I turn and start the other way. Again, more hedge.

Then the mist slips upward. Derek's and Cam's voices grow fainter. The mist turns into fingers and grabs at me, covers my mouth. Panic seizes me. I try to scream, but my voice is stifled. Slowly, the mist is dragging me down into the maze. I kick my feet, thrash my arms, but it's no use. The mist, or whatever it is, has complete hold over me.

Crammed in a wedge of hedge, the branches all turn to long fingers with jagged nails, pulling at my hair, my face. *Logan!* I scream in my mind.

Chapter 13

⸙ EYE-OPENER ⸙

*T*he mist forms a face in front of me: frightening, with jagged black holes for the eyes and mouth.

Stop your meddling or we will stop you, it croaks out. Branched fingers squeeze my throat, and I cough, choke. *It willna take much to silence you —*

"Let her go!"

Immediately, I'm released. Air sweeps into my lungs, and strong hands pull me from the hedge.

For a second, I'm confused. Strong hands? That voice had been Logan's. But when I stand, Serrus is steadying me. Logan stands right beside him.

"Are you all right?" Logan asks. He looks around, searching. "What happened?"

By now, the others have found their way to us. To Derek and Cam, it looks as if I'm just talking to Serrus.

"I don't know," I answer. "It was a warning, though." I look at Logan, and his features are almost see-through in the moonlight.

"Of what?" Serrus asks.

Logan's face is pinched with worry, the lines between his brows furrowed.

"A warning to stop meddling," I answer. "But I'm okay, really." I don't like being fussed over, and I certainly don't want everyone thinking I need rescuing. Although, what would have happened had Logan and Serrus not shown up? "I'm fine. I promise."

Logan's looking down at me, and his taut features and ticking jaw muscles say he doesn't believe me at all.

We hear the beep of a car horn — it's the twins' mom, coming to pick them up. We all slowly make our way out of the maze. Derek and Cam call out their good-byes and hurry toward their mom's car.

Once they leave, Serrus says to Logan, "Whatever's going on here, you seem to have the power to make it stop." He turns to me. "But if you need me, call my mobile."

Emma gives me a hug, making sure I'm all right. Then she climbs onto Serrus's motorbike and they drive away.

Logan walks with me to the jack-o'-lanterns, and I blow out all the candles. Glancing at the moon, I sigh. "Whatever happened to trick-or-treating and bobbing for apples?"

Logan stands close, and moves closer still. He looks down at me, and his gaze moves to my mouth, then back up to my eyes. "I dunno about all that," he says in his raspy brogue, "but if anything happens to you, gell . . ." He shakes his head, then holds my gaze. "I willna stand for it."

Butterflies beat the inside of my stomach. "I'm glad I met you, Logan Munro," I say.

We stand there, beneath the Samhain moon, and I find my legs turning into weak noodles.

"What Emma said to you in your room, upstairs," he asks, that charming smile tipping his mouth upward. "Is that so?"

I pretend not to know what he's referring to. "What do you mean?"

"Dunna play daft with me, lass," he says. "Do you?"

I knew he'd heard. "You were eavesdropping," I accuse. "Not cool."

His grin widens, and he steps closer. "Answer the question, Ivy Calhoun." His eyes twinkle in the moonlight. "And remember what a terrible liar you are before you give me an answer."

I blush clear to my roots, but he's right. "Yeah," I finally admit, and I meet his gaze. "I do feel that way."

Logan's smile widens. "Well," he says, after staring at me for a ridiculously long time, "let's go. This night, if you dunna mind, I'll be by your side whilst you sleep." He glances at the moon. "At least until the bewitching hour has passed."

"I won't argue with that," I answer. I grab my violin case and together we walk back.

Logan, ever the gentleman, waits outside my door while I get changed for bed. Then I call him in as I crawl beneath the covers. He makes himself comfortable, sitting at the foot of my bed, playing his flute. I love that only I can hear him.

With the music soothing me, I start reading *Enchanted Love* again. Eventually, I can't tell if Logan has stopped playing or not. I'm so fully into the incredible story. My heart beats faster and faster as the pages turn. It ends up that the American author in the book is able to reverse the enchantment on the Scottish men, and they come to life. She marries the clan leader and they all live together in the modern day. By midnight, I'm finished.

"Logan," I whisper.

He bolts upright off the floor. "What is it?" he asks worriedly.

"I'm okay, I'm okay," I reassure him. "But I have a feeling your cousins are more closely related to you than you think."

Logan cocks his head at me. "What do you mean?"

The book has given me an incredible notion. "What if," I begin, "we could reverse your . . . condition?"

Logan stares at me for a long while, and I wait. "You've gone mad," he declares.

"This book that your cousin's wife wrote?" I say, my voice shaking with excitement. "It's *their* story. It happened to them in real life. I'm sure of it!"

"What are you talkin' about, gell?" he asks.

I rub my face. "I don't know. Maybe I am crazy. But," I say, looking straight at Logan, "I think Ethan and his clansmen are old. Like, really old. Centuries old," I watch Logan's expression. "And I think Amelia met them in this century. And I think she . . . I don't know, undid their curse somehow." My eyes lock with his. "What if we could do the same with you?"

Logan's expression softens. "Ivy, darlin'," he says. "I'm no' cursed. I'm dead. There's no . . . undoin' it." He gives me a sad smile. "But I thank you for wantin' to try it."

I inhale, exhale. "You may be dead, but that doesn't mean you're not cursed. I'm still going to try to undo it. Why else would Amelia tell me to read this book with an open mind, and to call her as soon as I finish?"

"Well, for now . . ." Logan glances at the clock. "You've made it past the bewitching hour. School comes early in the morn and you'll have dark circles beneath those beautiful eyes of yours if you dunna get some rest."

I shake my head and smile. "Okay, okay. Good night, Logan."

I crawl beneath the covers and close my eyes, but in my head, thoughts run wild. As soon as I can, I'm talking to Amelia.

I call her the next morning, after Logan has wished me a good day and I've gone downstairs. I huddle in one of the hidden corridors off the kitchen and dial the number Amelia gave me. She answers on the first ring and sounds excited to hear from me.

"I loved your book," I tell her, then take a deep breath. "It's your story, isn't it? And I don't mean yours as in you wrote it. But yours. And Ethan's. And his clansmen."

Amelia laughs softly into the phone. "That's one open mind you got there, kiddo," she says. "And we definitely need to do this in person."

"Okay," I agree.

"But," she goes on, "I'm actually at the airport right now. I have to fly to the States for a short meeting with my editors. I'll only be a few days."

"Oh, man," I say under my breath.

Amelia laughs. "I promise, the second I get home, I'll call you. And I'll explain everything."

I sigh into the phone. "Thanks, Amelia."

The time passes while I wait for Amelia's return. I keep busy with my after-school music practice and homework and Logan. But as each day slips by, the Highlands become colder. A dreary gray canopy overhangs Glenmorrag. The trees are mostly barren and spindly. I haven't seen the sun in ages. I've lost track of time now. Other things occupy my mind.

Like the fact that I think I'm falling for a ghost. I admit this to no one, although Emma sees right through me. I did admit to Logan that I liked him, but even he doesn't realize how much. It makes no sense, even to me at times.

As my self-appointed guard, Logan gives me privacy, but he is never too far away. He's also my companion. We walk. We talk. When I go to the rectory to play my strings, he's there with me. He plays his flute for me, and there's nothing quite like being able to share our music.

And nothing strange or sinister has happened since Halloween.

On Friday afternoon, I'm walking through the great hall after school, planning to meet Logan upstairs, when I run slap into Grandmother Elizabeth.

Her small hand encircles my wrist like a band of iron. I'm so shocked at her strength, I gasp. It actually hurts where she's grabbing me, and I fight the urge to squeal.

"Where are you running to so fast, girl?" she asks. She shakes me, and my head snaps from the force of it. "Answer me!"

"Nowhere!" I exclaim, trying to yank away. "Let me go!"

"Are you snooping through my home?" she demands, in almost a growl. "Digging in drawers, going through rooms that are no' yours? Are you?"

"No!"

Logan appears and stares in horror. "Ivy! What's she doing?"

"Oh, there you are, Miss Ivy." Jonas's voice echoes up the corridor. Immediately, Elizabeth drops my arm. Jonas walks toward me.

Logan doesn't even bother disappearing.

"I thought you'd like some tea and cakes after school," he says. "If you'll meet me in the kitchen, then?" He turns politely to Elizabeth and nods. "Good afternoon, Lady MacAllister."

Grandmother Elizabeth, with only a foul glare, hurries away.

I'm trembling, I realize. I look at Logan.

He stares in the direction of old Elizabeth. He stares for a long time.

"Come, you two," Jonas says. "Ivy, why don't you take young Munro here to the movie room and relax. Watch a good picture. Aye?"

I nod. Elizabeth won't bother me in there — I've heard her telling Niall she thinks movies and television are a waste of time. "Good idea, Jonas. And thanks."

Inside the cozy movie room, Jonas sets down the tray of tea and meets my gaze with his weathered one. "She is not herself these days, I'm afraid. Be careful, child."

"I will," I assure him.

Jonas leaves us alone. Logan sits down on the sofa beside me.

"That," I say, still shaken, "was beyond weird. I mean, Elizabeth has always been harsh toward me, but she's never touched me before." I shake my head. "I couldn't break loose. She's ninety-something and strong as a bull."

Logan frowns. "Lady or no', I dunna like her laying

a hand on you, Ivy. You have to tell your mum and stepfather."

I sigh. "I don't want to bother them. Did I tell you they're expecting?"

Logan's eyes widen. "The laird and his lady are with child?"

"Aye," I answer, and Logan laughs. "I guess my mind has been on everything but that," I add.

"You said *aye*," he says.

I laugh, too. "I did. Now let's forget about everything for a while and get lost in a movie." I examine the DVD selection. "*Speed*. Oh, you've got to watch this one. Most excellent. A classic."

"*Speed*. I've never heard of such," Logan admits. "Shall we?"

"Have you ever watched a movie before?" I ask, sliding the DVD into its slot and picking up the remote.

"A few times I've caught the football game on the telly with Jonas or Ian, but no movies, I fear."

"Well, I know you've seen planes and cars and such," I say. "But this is seriously great Hollywood stuff here." I flick the movie onto play with the remote. I never thought I'd be having an afternoon movie date with a ghost.

"So there's a bomb beneath the bus," Logan says soon after, completely engrossed. "And Jack and Annie have to slide beneath it on the piece of flooring and dismantle it?"

"No," I correct. "To escape it. Just watch."

Watch Logan does. Intently. I stare at him as he stares at the flat screen. I can't get over how in awe of everything he is, like a little boy. When the doomed bus explodes into the side of a parked airplane, Logan's eyes widen and he jumps.

I can't help but laugh at his reactions.

By the end, he relaxes. He looks at me, smiles, and I nearly turn into a pool of mush on the sofa. When I turn off the TV, I realize that it's storming outside. Lightning flashes every few minutes, flickering into the room.

"You have so much to entertain you in this day and age," Logan marvels. "Music. Movies." He pauses. "What sort of music do you like to listen to on your box you plug into your ears?"

"My iPod? All sorts. Music from your day. My day. And in between." I pull it out of my hoodie pocket, turn it on, and hold a bud up to my ear. I select a Beethoven piece, one of my favorites, and hold it to Logan's ear. "See? I like this."

Logan listens for a moment, then smiles. "That sounds familiar. Fanciful, but familiar."

Next I choose "Walk This Way" by Aerosmith, and hold it to Logan's ear. He starts to grin. "That's . . . fast. Exciting. I like it."

Then I hit play on a piece I'd written and performed on an electric violin. Logan listens for a moment and then looks right at me, intently.

"That's your music," he says with confidence.

I smile. "It is."

Logan inches closer to me on the couch.

"I'm wondering about something," I ask.

One dark eyebrow lifts high, and his smile is wolfish. "Dare I ask what?"

I like the way his *r*'s roll, and sometimes he doesn't finish his *t*'s.

"Do you think you could feel my hand if I touch yours?" I venture.

"I dunna know," he says, his voice quiet. "Try."

Where my courage comes from, I have no idea. With a tentative hand, I slowly stretch my fingers toward him, close to his hand that rests casually against his knee. I note the strength in that hand, the veins that snake over the top and disappear beneath the sleeve of his white shirt. Veins that look as though they pump with life-sustaining blood. I think I've been mistaken, and that Logan actually is alive, sitting on the sofa next to me. A cute guy who's simply wearing nineteenth-century clothing for a play, maybe.

But it's just a fantasy.

My own hand hovers completely over his. My breath comes a bit faster. Then ever so slightly I graze the line of his knuckles with my fingertips.

I gasp as a surge of energy makes my skin tingle, and in surprise, we both look at each other. The sheer wonderment in Logan's silver eyes reflects the same in mine. Several words come to mind. Gratitude. Disbelief. Amazement.

If I'm anything at all, I'm determined to see Logan get another chance at life.

And that officially scares me. How can it not? Logan lived long ago, and his young life ended before it barely started. He's dead. And yet he makes me feel more alive than I've ever felt.

"What are you thinking, Ivy?" Logan asks quietly. He shifts closer to me.

Drawing a deep breath, I meet his gaze full on.

"I'm thinking how unreal all of this is. I'm thinking that, at one time, you were as alive as me, walking around, living your life. And then someone . . . stole it from you. And now here we are, together."

Logan lifts a hand, close to my jaw, his long fingers seemingly brushing a wisp of my hair aside. Of course, my hair doesn't move, but the motion of it, the intimacy of it, makes my heart leap.

"I'm glad it's you, Ivy. 'Twas meant for you to come here, to Glenmorrag." His smile vanishes, and his pur-poseful stare returns. "To me."

"I'm glad, too," I answer, and the smile that pulls at my own mouth is unstoppable. "So," I say, "where do we go from here?"

Logan doesn't answer. There is no easy answer. So we sit side by side, our hands almost touching, while outside the storm rages on.

Chapter 14

∾ CLUES ∾

It's Saturday morning. Amelia's due to arrive home this afternoon, and I'll hopefully get to see her tomorrow. Today, Emma and I are going into the village with Mom to stop by the library. Mom wants to check out a gazillion baby books, and Emma and I want to look up more about Glenmorrag's history. It was Emma who had the idea — she thought I might have missed some important clue about Logan or the castle in my quick research last time, and I wonder if she's right.

Logan stands with me outside the castle doors while I wait for Emma. Mom is getting ready inside.

"I'll go out and have a chat with Ian while you're gone," Logan is saying. "I've been neglecting the old guy lately." A slight grin curls up one corner of his mouth. "I canna fathom what's drawn my attention away so."

"Yeah, whatever," I say, smiling and fighting down my blush. "You'd better say hi to Emma first, though."

Logan grasps his heart. "Och. Two bonny lasses after me. Whatever tae do?"

"Your ego is getting out of control."

Just then, Emma pulls up on her scooter and removes her helmet. Wild ginger curls spring every which way.

"I'll bet that's fun tae ride on," Logan says, staring at the scooter. He smiles. "Mornin', Emma."

"Mornin', Logan," Emma says. She grins at me, proud of herself. "I think I'm getting used to seeing him."

"Aye, well, you two lovely ladies enjoy the village," Logan says. With a slight bow, he disappears.

"Okay," Emma whispers. "I can't get used to *that*."

"Listen," I tell her. "Amelia's coming back today. I can't wait to talk to her."

"Aye." Emma's finished *Enchanted Love* as well, and we've compared our theories. Emma agrees that the story must match Amelia's life, fantastical as it seems. "If that book she wrote has as much meanin' as we think, she may have the answer to all of this."

Gosh, I hope so.

"Oh, hi, Emma," Mom says, coming out the door. She's looking very pretty in her bright pink hat, matching scarf, and dark coat. "You girls ready?"

"Hi, Lady M.," Emma says. "Love the hat."

"Strap that seat belt on," I warn Emma as we get into the car. "Seriously. Ride of your life."

"That's not nice, Ivy," Mom says, laughing.

"But it's the total truth," I answer.

With Em's eyes wide as saucers at Mom's UK driving, we arrive at the village. It's gray out, the persistent slip of mist settling over the water. We park by the seawall, and I open my door. Several fishing boats are anchored in the bay, bobbing within the white hazy vapor. In the distance, something bongs a buoy, and it echoes off the stone buildings.

"Now that's just creepy," Mom says as we get out of the car, and I think, *You don't know creepy, Mom.*

Once inside the library, Mom ensconces herself in the parenting section while Emma and I go straight to the local-history section.

"Here's something," Emma says, pulling a tome from the shelf. "Medieval Glenmorrag." She flips the book open and scans the pages. "Aye, this one's a keeper. Lots of stuff in here."

We go through the short line of books on the village's history, find a couple more to check out, then head to the computer room.

"I don't even know what I'm looking for," I say, "but maybe there's something on microfilm."

"Like, something that happened in the village? Or something about strange events at the castle?" Emma asks.

"Exactly."

Finally we get the microfilm and hook up everything on the machine. I scroll through the old pages of the *Glenmorrag Gazette*. It casts a white glow in the darkened room. Nothing too interesting or strange seems to jump out over the years. I go back five years, ten, twenty. . . .

"Hey," Emma says, reading over my shoulder, and I pause. "The Glenmorrag storm, 1983. I remember my mum talking about it. Huge storm o' the elements, she said. Lightning. Thunder. Hail, even. And winds of hurricane proportion. Lightning struck my gran's croft and burned it to the ground."

"Wow," I say as I read. "It all occurred in one day. November 20, 1983." I'm not sure why this storm is important but somehow I can't look away from the article.

"What are you reading, sweetie?"

Emma gasps. I jump in my seat and turn to face Mom.

"Mom! You scared us!" I take a calming breath.

Mom laughs. "Sorry guys. So what are you reading?"

"Nothing, just some old Glenmorrag history," I say. I turn off the computer and glance at the stack of books tucked under her arm. "Ready?"

My mom beams. "Yes I am! It's been a long time since you were a baby. I've lots to read up on."

I laugh and shake my head. "I seriously doubt things have changed all that much, Mom."

"Well, I did do okay with you, I suppose," Mom says teasingly. "Raised a violin prodigy and all."

I smile at Mom as Emma laughs. "Maybe you'll have another one?" Emma suggests.

Mom winks at Emma and nudges me. "There can be only one Ivy. My first baby." I feel a flush of joy at her words. "How are things going with practice for the Strings festival?" she asks me.

As we discuss my music, I realize how much I miss my mom. Again, part of me wants to tell her about everything weird I've experienced at Glenmorrag. The freezer, the raven, the hedge maze, the choking. Logan. Especially Logan.

But I barely believe that he's real myself — no way would she. Or anyone else for that matter . . . except Ian, and Jonas, of course. And Emma. Serrus.

And Amelia, along with the entire Munro clan.

I guess I have a larger support group than I thought.

We check out all of Mom's parenting books and the ones on Glenmorrag Emma and I found. Loaded with books, we leave.

Once we're back at Glenmorrag, Mom brings the baby books to Niall in the sitting room. I open the hall closet for Emma and me to hang our coats. As I close the door, Elizabeth is standing there.

"What did you do to the window upstairs?" she asks me. With her lips tightly pulled, her brows furrowed, she awaits my answer.

I send Emma a hasty look. "I didn't do anything to it," I answer. "A raven flew into it and broke it."

Elizabeth's eyes narrow.

Even though the MacAllister matriarch intimidates me, I don't look away.

The old woman's stare never leaves mine, even for a second. "Birds aren't the only things that can go through windows," she says.

A small gasp escapes Emma's throat.

Elizabeth smiles, and with her forefinger and thumb, she twirls that gaudy ring she always wears.

"You're right," I say, and I continue to stare at her, unblinking.

Elizabeth's eyes turn to pure ice. "Watch your tongue, girl," she says. "Or you'll be taught a lesson you'll not forget." Without another word, she turns on her little heels and struts across the hall and disappears into the shadows.

A breath escapes me.

"I fancy a girl with backbone. Truly."

I cover my mouth with my hand to quiet my squawk of surprise seeing Logan appear out of nowhere.

"You've got to start giving me a warning before you just pop up," I say. "Seriously. You're going to give me a heart attack."

"Och," Logan says, "strong lass like yourself can withstand a little surprise here and again, aye?" He glances in the direction Elizabeth disappeared. "The old girl truly doesna fancy you. She threatened you, Ivy. Right in front of Emma here."

"Me thinks the old bird wants tae shove Ivy out the window," Emma says angrily. "The look in her eyes?" She shudders. "Possessed."

I sigh. "No kidding. Anyway, let's go find Ian."

"Why?" Logan and Emma both say at once.

"I'd like to ask him if he remembers anything about that storm," I answer, looking at Emma. To Logan, I add, "A big multielemental storm happened here, about thirty years ago. Ian's been here for forty. Surely he'll remember."

"Ian's out in the maze," Logan says. He thinks for a minute. "I dunna recall such a storm. I must've been wanderin' elsewhere at the time."

Emma's phone rings. Pulling it from her pocket, she says, "It's me mum. I'll be just outside." She heads for the door, letting it close behind her.

I pull my hat snug over my ears, and reach for the door handle myself. But Logan swears under his breath.

"What's wrong?" I ask him.

Logan lowers his head close to mine. "Just know this, Ivy Calhoun," he begins. "If I werena a ghost I would open all doors for you, properly." He frowns. "As it is, you must open them for yourself."

A smile spreads across my face. "It's okay, Logan. Really."

" 'Twill have to be, aye?" he answers. "I'm stuck in this lifeless body."

Somberness grips me, and I think it grips Logan as well. For a moment, we're silent. In the great hall, sunk in the recessed shadows, we stand face-to-face.

"Being a ghost hasna bothered me so much," he whispers. "Until now." He leans into me, our mouths close. "Until you."

I literally feel tingles on my lips. My heart skips a beat.

I want him to kiss me. More than anything. But he can't. I can't.

A small smile tips up the corner of Logan's mouth. "We'd best get to that maze," he says softly. The look on my face must reveal puzzlement, because he chuckles. "Ian? Questions? Storm?"

"Right!" I say, and struggle not to slap myself. Has a ghost really made me so loopy? I slide past Logan and open the front door. The blast of cold air hits me in the face and I breathe it in, welcome it.

"What's wrong wi' you, Ivy?" Emma says, standing on the last step. "You're as pale as a sheet."

Behind me, Logan laughs softly, and I feel my cheeks turn crimson.

"If you were alive, I'd elbow you in the gut," I say to Logan, heading down the graveled path.

"I know you would," Logan answers, walking beside me.

"What'd I miss?" Emma asks, looking between me and Logan. "Somethin' good, wasna it?"

Logan just chuckles, and we all continue on toward the maze.

Waves crash against the rock Glenmorrag is built upon, the sound rumbling through me as we make our way across the bailey. Within a few moments, we arrive at the maze and find Ian, trimming a section of the hedge. He glances up at our arrival.

"Och, look at ya," he says, pushing the old soft hat perched on his head back a ways. "'Tis an odd thing indeed, seein' you, boy, with another living soul besides myself, or Jonas," Ian says. "Much less two lasses." He laughs. "What can I do you for this fine Highland afternoon?"

"Do you remember a big storm that happened here?" I ask.

"The one in '83," Emma offers.

Ian nods. "Aye. 'Twas a wild storm, that day. Crumbled a goodly amount of the rectory." He scratches his head. "I even remember that poor Lady Elizabeth, she was caught in the storm. Had to be carried in by the servants." He takes a couple of clips at the hedge, then meets my gaze in particular. "'Twas odd, too, how the next day, she was changed. Up till that day, she'd been a fine, chipper lady. But after that storm, an icy glaze covered her eyes and she's been cold ever since."

A chill goes through me. Elizabeth? She'd been nice before the storm? Why? How?

Before I can ask more, my cell phone rings. Amelia Munro's name lights up the screen, and I look at Logan and Emma. "It's Amelia! Sorry, Ian, I have to take this call!"

Chapter 15

"I'm back now, and you must come over together," Amelia says. "We've a lot to talk about. And Ethan wants to meet Logan."

"He's anxious to meet you all, too," I say. "But there's a problem."

"What's that?"

I sigh. "Logan tried to hitch a ride in my stepdad's car and he sort of, I don't know, his body couldn't keep up. He just popped out of it."

"Hmm," Amelia says. "Let me talk to Ethan. I'll text you later, okay?"

"Sounds good to me," I answer. "Thanks, Amelia."

"You bet, kiddo."

Just then, Serrus's motorcycle pulls up the gravel

drive. Pulling off his helmet, he sets it on the handlebar and comes toward me. At this point, Logan and Emma are walking away from the maze to join us.

"Hey, guys," Serrus says, then turns to Logan. "Cousin."

"Cousin, yourself," Logan responds with a grin. "How is it to ride that big metal beast?" Logan inclines his head toward the motorcycle.

Serrus smiles. "From what I hear, if 'tis left up to Ivy here, you'll one day be able to know that for yourself." He grins at me. "You're all the talk up at the Munro tower."

"Oh, boy," I say, and Serrus laughs.

"All good talk, I promise," Serrus assures. "So what are you all up to?"

Quickly, we fill him in on our findings at the library, the storm, and what Ian says about Elizabeth. Serrus whistles low.

"Aye, the Munros talk about that storm every so often," Serrus says. "Ethan swears it had roots in the dark arts."

I feel my ears prick up. "What do you mean?"

" 'Twas black magic that caused such a change in the elements," he says.

"Well, I'm going over to talk to Amelia as soon as possible," I say, and look at both Serrus and Emma. "You guys want to come?"

"Aye," they say in unison.

"Ethan's trying to figure out a way for Logan to get there," I explain, glancing at Logan. "Last time, it didn't work out."

"He will," Serrus says. "When Ethan Munro decides something, he doesna turn loose until he's seen it happen."

That comforts me. I want Logan to go. He has to.

Sure enough, later that evening, after Emma and Serrus have gone home and I'm getting ready for bed with Logan outside my door, I get a text from Amelia.

Ethan has drawn a walking map for Logan, and I've e-mailed it to you. It's not on the modern roads, but a path Logan would have walked during the time he was alive. Ethan says he should leave at daybreak. Once he's here, I'll come and get you.

I hurriedly open my door and hustle Logan inside, explaining Amelia's text.

"Aye, 'tis worth a try, indeed," Logan agrees.

I check my e-mail and print out Ethan's map. Logan and I go over it together. Logan knows exactly where the tower is and what path to take. He'll depart before daybreak so he'll have enough time to get there.

Before Logan leaves my room for the night, he gives me a long look. "Thank you."

I cock my head. "For what?"

His eyes soften, like liquid mercury in an old thermometer. "For what you're doin' for me."

Without breaking our gaze, I smile. "I can't think of anything else I'd rather be doing."

He smiles back. "Good night, Ivy Calhoun. 'Til the morn."

I remember how much I wanted him to kiss me earlier in the day, and that same ache returns. I look down, reminding myself that it can't be. At least, not now.

"Good night," I say softly.

It's late — nearly midnight — and I'm lying in my bed, covers pulled up to my chin, reading *The Ghost of Dibble*

Hollow. I jump at the sound of something falling onto my floor, and I peer into the shadows beyond my lamplight. I see nothing. That is, until my eyes light on an object just in front of my dresser. Setting my book aside, I crawl from the bed, ease over to the thing, and crouch down. I pick it up. I blink.

It's the rowan bark. From the raven's beak. How the heck did it get back in here?

Lightning flashes, illuminating my room in an eerie milky glow.

And far away, as if on the opposite side of the castle, I hear a soft cry.

My skin tingles, and I strain to listen.

Again I hear it. A woman crying out. It's not the peacocks. It almost sounds like — Mom?

Just then, my bedside lamp goes out; a frosty chill descends upon the room. Mist thickens and swirls around me. Goose bumps rise on my skin.

"Logan," I say, in almost a whisper. I don't realize how scared I am until I barely hear my voice. "Logan!"

He immediately appears, looks at me, the icy room, and the rowan in my hand. His face grows angry. "Ivy, leave," he says. "Now!"

I drop the rowan, run to the door, and grab the knob. It is stuck in place. "It won't open," I say, twisting it back and forth. "Logan, it's stuck!"

"Open the bloody door!" Logan commands to . . . someone. Or something. "Now!"

Just then, a shadowy figure emerges from the mist. Its face . . . a jagged open mouth with sharp teeth and black holes for eyes. The rest of the figure is a blur. But it lunges at me, and I dart away.

Logan leaps at the figure and my eyes widen as his hands encircle the figure's neck. With a forceful fling, Logan throws it against the wall. When I blink, the figure has arms, hands, and legs. It strikes at Logan, and he fights it off.

I spy my iron poker in the corner. I run toward it, grab it, and just as Logan throws the figure against the wall again, I swing the poker at it. Hard.

It instantly vanishes.

At once, normal temperature returns to the room, the bedside lamp turns on, and a click sounds at the door.

Remembering the sound of my mother crying out, I twist the doorknob and it opens. I take off down the corridor.

"Ivy, wait!" I hear Logan call behind me.

But I don't wait.

"Follow me!" I call after him.

I reach my mother's room. I'm about to open the door when Elizabeth emerges. Her eyes narrow.

"Your mother has fallen ill and needs to rest. Return to your chambers, Ivy," she commands.

"I want to see my mom," I say, now frantic. What's wrong with my mother? I feel a stab of panic. Or is something wrong with the baby inside her?

"Return to your chambers, young lady," Elizabeth says again. "You can see your mother when she is feeling better."

"I'll see her now —"

Niall steps from the room, his impossible height towering over me. He glances first at his grandmother, then at me.

"Ivy, your mother is simply experiencing morning sickness at night," he says. "Not an uncommon symptom of pregnancy, I hear." He's worried, I can tell. "She's just fallen back to sleep. I'll watch over her. I promise."

"Ivy," Logan, in his invisible state, whispers in my ear. "I've just looked in on her. She is indeed sleeping. Come with me," he says. "Just walk away."

"I want to see her when she wakes up," I say to Niall, and he gives me a single nod.

I glare at Elizabeth, turn, and leave.

Down the darkened corridor Logan and I walk toward the stairs. We're just about to round the corner to the steps when Jonas appears. In his long, blue woolen robe and striped pajamas, he looks like something out of a Charles Dickens novel. The only thing missing is a long, pointy nightcap and a candle.

"Ah, young Ivy," he says, and glances at Logan. "Master Munro," he whispers. "Why are you up in the middle of the night, lass?" he asks me.

"You mean after some crazy spirit thing attacked me and fought Logan in my room? I heard my mother cry out," I answer, frustrated. "Elizabeth and Niall won't let me see her." I search Jonas's expression, wondering if he knows anything. "He says she has morning sickness."

Jonas's eyes widen. "Och, lass. Something attacked you? Are you hurt?"

I shake my head. "No. I'm fine." I glance at Logan. "I had a lot of help." I look back at Jonas. "But my mom. Morning sickness?"

"Bloody morning sickness," Jonas says quietly. "Aye, can be quite vicious." His kind eyes are reassuring. "I promise I'll keep a listen out for her, dear. Don't you worry." Shooting a look at Logan, he lifts one silver eyebrow. "Lad, what was it that tried to attack Ivy?"

"'Twas something I could physically put my hands on," Logan says. "I believe 'twas another spirit."

"Oh, dear. What happened before it appeared?" Jonas asks.

Quickly, I tell him about the rowan bark, the temperature drop, the locked door.

"Rowan." Jonas slips a quick look at Logan.

"Aye, rowan," Logan says.

"It must be burned. Toss it out your window, and I'll do the deed tonight," Jonas instructs.

I thank Jonas and start up the steps. I don't know if everything is now starting to really get to me, but the walls seem to close in on me. If I stare long enough at the aged stone, it seems to breathe. My gaze fixes onto the lone straight-backed chair farther down the hall until I get to my room. I fling open the door and hurry inside.

"Ivy," Logan says softly. "Stop. Please."

I don't, though, until I've grabbed the rowan bark and thrown it out the window. Within minutes, Jonas appears on the stone walkway below and sets the bark on fire, just as he promised. I stare at the smoldering wood until it's nothing more than a pin-dot ember.

I breathe a sigh of relief. For tonight, maybe, I can rest easy. But whatever dark spirit exists in the castle — I think it's still here.

Chapter 16

*M*y eyes crack open in the morning. I want to call Logan's name but then I remember he's gone. On his way to the Munros. Fear and excitement course through me. I hope he makes it.

I notice a strange something streaming across my bedroom. I haven't seen it in . . . days. It looks foreign. Out of place in the dreariness of Glenmorrag.

Sunlight.

Scrambling from the plaid confinement of my draped bed, I hurry to the picture window. Early-morning mist drifts across the ground, but high above, through the clouds, a break, allowing a golden beam to burn its way straight to me. I press my face to the glass. No warmth — the pane is still freezing. But there is light.

Hurriedly, I dress. Jeans. Thermal. Button-up shirt. Boots. I want to be totally ready when Amelia texts me. So much to discuss today. So much hope.

On the second-floor landing, I run into Niall.

"Och, Ivy," he says, and his face is tired. Haggard. Like he's been up all night. "You poor lasses. If you all have to endure this . . . morning sickness when you carry a babe, God bless ya."

"Is Mom okay?" I ask, and peer toward the door.

He nods. "She's finally getting some rest. I'm on my way to get her some more ginger ale in the village." He inclines his head. "Grandmother is in with her now."

My stomach drops. That doesn't make me feel any better about Mom's condition.

"Walk wi' me, Ivy," Niall says, and I agree. We both head up the corridor. "I know Gran hasna quite taken to you," he says. "She's a dodgy old thing lately." He glances at me as we walk. "Please overlook her bad behavior. She's like an old dog at this point. No teachin' her any new tricks."

I'm now convinced Niall doesn't know just how awful his grandma has been to me. More than awful. Not . . . right. And I don't have enough evidence to show him.

"It's okay," I say instead. "I just want my mom to get better."

Niall stops me, his hand on my shoulder. "I'd never let anything happen to her."

Looking at the sincerity in my stepdad's eyes, I believe him. I think about how Logan vowed to protect me. And I realize Niall might not be so bad after all.

"Thank you," I say.

"So where are you off to today?" he asks as we continue down the stairs.

"Amelia Munro is picking me up," I say. "Serrus and Emma are going over there, too."

"Aye? What for?"

My mind races. *Oh, you know. Looking for ways to bring my dead boyfriend back to life. To figure out how he died, and what's haunting Glenmorrag.* "Movies." I shrug. "They have an enormous movie room."

"Have a fine time," he says. "Dunna worry too much about your mum."

"I'll try," I say.

Zipping up my coat, I head outside. I'm a little nervous. Scratch that. I'm a lot nervous. About leaving Mom. About whether or not Logan makes it to the Munros okay.

And what's going to happen once I get to the Munro Tower House.

My cell phone vibrates. I grab it. It's Emma.

Did he make it? she asks.

Haven't heard yet, I respond.

Bollocks. Well let me know asap xo

I take a walk to the cliffs. The roar of the sea, paired with the wind, is deafening. The gulls manage to screech above it, though, and I watch them swoop and dive. Glancing over my shoulder, I stare at the castle behind me. It's so . . . huge.

And suddenly I feel very much alone.

I'm used to Logan being at my side.

My phone vibrates again. If it's Emma, I'll strangle her.

It's Amelia.

He's made it! Girl, he is cute! I'll be over to pick you up in thirty minutes.

Yes! I text back, laughing right out loud. **I'm waiting in the drive.** I'm so excited I can barely stand still.

Within twenty-five minutes, Amelia pulls up in an old white Rover. I can see her wide smile from where I stand. She slows, and I pull open the door and climb in.

"Now," Amelia says as she drives, "we've got approximately twenty-three minutes before we arrive at the tower, so why don't you tell me every little detail about how you first met Logan, and everything that has transpired since." She gives me a sly look. "Don't leave one juicy detail out, either, Ivy Calhoun. I mean it."

I laugh. "I will, but first," I ask, "did it all really happen? Just the way you wrote it in *Enchanted Love*?"

Amelia gives me a quick glance and a smile. "Every last detail. Including Ethan's proposal at the airport." She laughs. "I gotta hand it to him. Having passengers get off the plane and walk up to me in the airport and each hand me a single rose and a card with one word on it, all put together saying *Will you wed me, lass?* is pretty freaking clever." She winks at me. "Don't you think?"

"Well, especially since you'd thought you'd lost him forever," I say. "That story was, is . . . amazing beyond belief. When you had gone home to Charleston, and your friend brought you that postcard from Scotland, and it had that picture on it of the yew tree? With *Ethan loves Amelia, by the by* . . . carved into it?" I sigh. "Oh my gosh," I say. "Makes you sincerely believe in magic — and miracles."

"It truly does," Amelia agrees.

"So is that really how you brought him back to life?" I ask. "Reciting that old Gaelic incantation, over a burning scrap of yew wood?" I'm hopeful. "Can I do the same for Logan?"

Amelia keeps her eyes on the road. "I looked up the spell yesterday and unfortunately I don't think it will work on Logan. He's not in between death and life the way Ethan and his kinsmen were. I'm not sure if there's any way to reverse his current state." She pauses. "I'm sorry, Ivy."

I fall silent, a lump forming in my throat. I should have known it was too much to wish for. But still . . .

"It's okay," Amelia assures me. "There's still much to talk about. We don't quite know what Logan's story is. But," she adds brightly, "why don't *you* finally tell me how you met Logan?"

This is just the right question to lift my mood. I start at the beginning, when I first spied Logan Munro in the castle kitchen.

When we pull into the Munros' long, shadowy drive lined with Scotch pines, I'm still talking away. Amelia parks the Rover, and I finish with what had happened the night before.

"That awful thing in your room sounds terrifying." She shakes her head and gets out, and I follow. "How'd you know to use something made of iron?"

I close the car door. "Emma. I carried it around for a while."

"Aye, the lass knows how to look after herself," a familiar voice says behind me.

I turn, and Logan is standing a few feet away. I hurry up to him and stop just before plowing through him. I realize I'm about to give him a hug, as if that's the perfectly natural response. It is. Just not to a ghost.

"Hey," I say, excited and flustered all at once. "You made it."

Logan gives a nod. "I did indeed."

Words in a language I don't understand rise from the steps of the tower house — or keep, as Amelia corrected me earlier.

I look behind Logan to see Ethan and his cousins all gathered there. Grinning. When I glance back at Logan, he grins, too, and shrugs.

"Family," he says.

At that moment, Serrus pulls up on his motorcycle,

and Emma's on the back. They park, and we head inside. Again, we all gather in the great hall.

I take a seat on the same mossy-green velvet chair I did before. Logan sits next to me. The guys all pile in on sofas and recliners. Amelia sits across from me, perched on a big wooden coffee table.

"Ivy, I want you to tell Ethan and the guys what you told me on the way over," Amelia says. I pause, not wanting to tell all these men — with Logan there, no less, about my growing feelings for Logan. "The dark presence and weird goings-on," she clarifies, and I give her a grateful smile.

So I begin. Ethan and the other Munros listen intently. I tell them of being pushed into the freezer, nearly choking, the raven and the rowan bark, the hideous figure in the maze, and in my room. The Munros all exchange looks, silent.

"I wonder," I say out loud, "if this spirit, whatever it is, has something to do with Logan and his murder?"

"No' tae scare you, lass," Aiden speaks up, "but it sounds tae me as though the living is controlling something . . . unliving."

"And no' tae scare you even worse, but who's tae say my cousin here was murdered?" Ethan says.

Shock creeps over me, and I feel the blood rush from my face. Ethan's right. What if Logan simply had a tragic accident?

"I can see smoke risin' from atop your head at all those thoughts, lass," Ethan says. "But what I meant was, who's tae say young Logan here is dead at all? He doesna recall dyin'."

I blink. I look at Logan, then at Amelia, then back to Ethan.

"All I'm sayin' is, we have tae keep all doors open here," Ethan goes on. "You know our tale." He sweeps the hall, indicating his kinsmen. "You know we were accursed. Ghostly during the daylight hours and the night. Only during that space of the gloaming time did we gain our bodies and become mortal."

I nod, amazed that what sounds like legend is so real.

"'Twasn't till I fell in love with Amelia here and we did the incantation with the yew bark, that the curse was lifted," Ethan goes on. He squints at Logan. "Do you remember anything at all, lad? Anything that can close the gap from before and after?"

I look up at Logan, and I see his brows knit together in thought. He shakes his head. "Nay."

"Maybe showing him the portrait room will jog his memory," Amelia says. She stands and looks at first me, then Logan. "Come on."

Amelia leads the way. Up the spiral staircase, we all trek to the library. The lights are off, but there is sunshine streaming through the windows, casting brilliant shafts across the wood-planked floor. Amelia walks over to the wall of portraits, Logan right behind her.

"My mother," Logan whispers, and steps closer to the portrait of Mirrah Munro. Longing fills his eyes, and he reaches up with a hand, as if to touch it, then pulls it back to his side. "I miss her. She was a good mum."

"Anything else?" Ethan asks from behind us.

Logan's gaze moves to the next portrait. "Uncle Patrick." His gaze lingers there, searching, studying every detail. He cocks his head and draws closer, but doesn't say a word. He stares for a long time. He moves closer to the portrait, then backs up.

"What is it?" I ask, staring at the image of Patrick. Something bothers me about it, too, and just like before, I can't place what it is.

Everyone in the room moves closer. We're all staring at the portrait now. Even Emma is studying it.

"'Tis the ring," Logan finally says, and looks directly at me. "'Tis the same bloody ring Elizabeth MacAllister wears now." His eyes search mine. "She's always twisting it."

My eyes widen as I stare at the ring on Patrick's finger. "You're right," I whisper.

It's the same bright ruby ring, right down to the intricate setting. My heart begins to thud. That was what I had noticed before, but it hadn't registered. I look at Logan, then Ethan. "What does that mean?"

Ethan squints at the ring, too. "I dunno," he says. "It doesna make much sense. Why would a present-day MacAllister have the ring of a long-dead Munro?"

"I'm not sure," I answer. "But that's exactly what I'm going to find out."

Chapter 17

∽ THE KISS ∽

We spend the rest of the day at the Munro keep. After lunch, Amelia, Ethan, and the rest of the clan walk us out to the forest behind the old tower house.

The sun has disappeared once more, and gloom and mist settle over the Highlands. The air is still sweet, though, and cold and crisp as we follow the Munros down a well-beaten path. Logan walks beside me, and we exchange several glances. His eyes glimmer like quicksilver.

The deeper into the forest we go, the more shadowy it becomes. Long wisps of mist slip over the ground and through the trees towering overhead. The spicy scent of Scotch pine fills the air, and somewhere above, a raven caws.

Finally, at the end of the path, a small clearing.

In that clearing, a tree. An ancient, gnarled tree. And as we grow closer, I see an inscription, carved deep into the wood.

Ethan loves Amelia. By the by . . .

"Och," Emma breathes. "Just like in the book."

The guys all erupt into laughter.

"Exactly like the book," Amelia says, and casts her gaze to me and Logan. "Ethan carved that in the fourteenth century. Anything's possible, Ivy."

Ethan pulls his wife toward him and kisses the top of her head. Even though Amelia is tall, Ethan towers over her.

They make the perfect pair.

Ethan slowly releases Amelia, then steps up to the tree and pulls a Swiss Army knife from his pocket.

"You know what sort of tree this is, aye, cousin?" he says to Logan.

Logan nods. " 'Tis a yew."

Ethan carves off a small branch with his blade. "And you know about yew, dunna you, boy?"

"Aye," Logan says. "Like the rowan is cursed, the yew is opposite. 'Tis protective. Mystically so."

Ethan whittles off four slivers, smooths them with the side of his knife, and hands two to me, one to Emma, and one to Serrus. "Keep it with you always, and secure it so it doesna fall out. Just in case." He then walks to Logan and looks down at him. Silver eyes meet silver eyes. "Me and my kin, we were out o' place in time," Ethan says. "Once our enchantment had been broken, there was nowhere else for us tae be, save here, in this time. We'd been missing in history all those centuries." He shakes his head, but his eyes never leave Logan's. "I dunna know your destiny, cousin, but no matter what it might be, we're your kin. You've a place here, if you want it. Live or dead."

A sigh escapes Logan's throat, but I'm pretty sure only I hear it. "Thank you," he says, and looks down at me. "I've got tae make it safe for Ivy at Glenmorrag first."

A slow smile, so much like Logan's, lifts the corners of Ethan's mouth. "I'd expect nothin' less of you, boy," he says. "You're a Munro, after all."

Logan's smile matches Ethan's. "That I am."

Ethan turns his silvery gaze on me. "Lass, if you need anything at all, you call."

"Thanks," I say. "I will."

Logan takes his ancient footpath across the wood back to MacAllister land, and I pray he makes it there without any problems. Serrus and Emma say good-bye and head off on Serrus's bike. Amelia drives me back to Glenmorrag, and on the way we talk about Charleston, fried shrimp and crab cakes, and hot, sticky, balmy nights of the South. I tell her about my dad, and since Serrus had already bragged about my music, she makes me promise to come back to the Munro keep to play for everyone. I do.

Just as I step into the foyer of Glenmorrag Castle, the drizzle begins again. Inside the great hall, the tall suit of armor is a little more terrifying than when the sunshine was streaming in upon the metal earlier.

As soon as I close the door behind me and turn around, I see Niall is there.

"Is my mother okay?" I ask, noticing the worry on his face.

"She was awake earlier," he says, his brows furrowed, "and asked me to let you know she will be fine." He scrubs his jaw with his hand. "But I couldna find you."

"Oh," I say. "Sorry. I stayed at the Munros for a while."

Niall studies me. Half of his face is cast in shadow. I can't help but wonder if he knows anything about his grandmother, or the ring. Maybe I should ask him?

Before I can, though, he says, "The physician came by, and warned us that your mum is highly susceptible to germs at this point. It's probably best if she doesn't have too many visitors to her bedside, Ivy." He holds my gaze. "Trust me, girl. I'll take ever so much great care of her and the baby. I promise. This all has me baffled, too."

I fight back tears. I hate that Mom is sick. "Okay. But please tell her I love her. And when she wakes up again, I just want to . . . stand at the door and tell her myself. Okay?"

"Aye," he answers. "I will do that." He turns to leave.

I go upstairs and pace my room, worrying about Mom, until Logan at last returns. He has successfully taken the path back from the Munro keep, and I'm not sure I've ever been happier to see him. The moment he appears in my room, I announce, "Let's go find Jonas. He might have some answers about the ring we saw in the portrait."

"Aye," he agrees, and we go.

Jonas is preparing supper in the kitchen, and in a low voice, I start out by asking him if he has a memory of

Elizabeth not being so cruel. I want to see if he gives the same answers as Ian, about the storm. Or if he mentions the ring.

Jonas stares at me, his watery blue eyes soft, alert. But there's something else there, too. I recognize it. It's fear.

"Let me think. It was probably about thirty years ago. Funny," he muses to himself. "Seems like ever since that storm hit, she's changed." He looks at me. " 'Twas overnight, or so it seems."

"What about the ring?" I share a look with Logan.

"That big ruby ring she wears? Aye. She actually found it the night of the storm. The moment she slipped it on, she didna want to take it off. " He looks at me. "Passing odd."

"Logan's uncle, his mom's brother, had that same ring," I admit.

"Are you positive, lad?" Jonas asks Logan.

Logan nods. "Aye."

"It means something," I say, and lean against the counter. "The storm. The ring. Her behavior change." I look at Logan. "It's all linked."

Logan nods. "Aye, I'm sure of it."

"We'll find out. I promise. Let's go call Ethan." I look at Jonas. "Thanks for helping us." We turn to leave.

"Miss Ivy?" he says as we're almost to the door. We both turn.

"Please, dear," he warns. "You know not where your questioning will lead. There are dangers lurking." He pauses. "Take care."

"We will," Logan says firmly.

Jonas gives a single nod.

Logan and I walk out in silence.

"Let's go to the rectory," Logan suggests. "Bundle up, get your instrument, and come. Call Ethan and Amelia from there. Play for me. You've got tae practice anyway."

I look at the ghostly boy before me and know there's nothing more I can do until we talk to the Munros. And there's nothing more I'd rather do right now than be with Logan. His mystery has lasted almost two centuries. Another evening won't hurt.

"Okay," I answer, smiling despite myself.

"Meet me there in fifteen minutes," Logan says excitedly. "Not a second earlier!"

With one brow lifted in question, I stare at him.

"Promise me, not a second earlier?" he says.

"All right, then," I answer. "See you in fifteen."

Logan's smile stretches from one ear to the other. "Wait! Make it twenty!"

And as he fades, the whites of his teeth are the last to disappear. Sort of his trademark, I guess. I like it.

I have no idea what he's up to, but I know one thing.

I'm falling for him. Hard.

I turn and run up the steps to my room. I'll grab my strings and my phone and come back down to put on my coat. At the second-floor landing, though, I pause, and glance down the dim corridor. Toward my mother's room. Before I realize it, my feet are moving in that direction. It's then that I notice the shadows are long in the hall, obscuring the antiques and medieval works of art on the walls. It's nothing but darkness. My pace slows. At once, something shifts in the shadows. Rather, the shadows move. Panic seizes me. My vision becomes hazy, my legs weak. . . .

"Ivy? Is that you?"

Niall is looking out of Mom's room. Elizabeth stands beside him, peering at me. My eyes fly to that hideous ring she's twisting around and around her finger.

"Yes, it's me," I say, taking a deep breath. I glance at that particular spot in the shadows. Nothing is there. Maybe I was having a panic attack. "I was hoping Mom could —"

"Not right now," Elizabeth says sharply. "She has just drifted off to sleep after a restless bit. The last thing she needs is more worry."

I glare at Elizabeth. "The last thing she needs is you," I say, not caring if I sound disrespectful. "I'll see my mother. When she wakes up, I'll be back —"

"Ivy, sweetie?" my mom calls out.

I poke my head into the room. "Hi, Mom. How are you feeling?"

She is propped up in bed, her face wan. This seems like something more than morning sickness. Deep concern twists in my gut.

"Like a weakling," she answers, trying to smile, "but I'm okay. Honest, sweetheart. Niall's looking after me like a champion."

"Okay," I say. But she looks . . . wasted away. Like the life is being sucked right out of her. I draw a deep breath to hide my fear. "I love you."

"I love you, baby," she answers. "We'll chat tomorrow. Okay?"

"Okay, Mom." I'm almost in tears now.

Cutting between Niall and Elizabeth, I quit the corridor and head upstairs. I'm shaking, I'm so mad and unnerved, and all I want right now is to find Logan at the rectory. And call the Munros. I hurry into my room, grab my case and cell phone, and leave.

Downstairs, I pull on my coat, then head out. I'm not even sure if it's been twenty minutes, or longer. For a moment, I stop, allowing the cold damp air to rush over me in the courtyard. I take several deep breaths in, and exhale. Above me, hidden within the canopy of trees, the peacocks stare down at me. Their soft cooing floats on a breeze, barely audible.

Something had been hiding in the shadows on the second floor. Who, or what, had it been? I'll call Amelia and Ethan, and tell them what's happened. They'll know what to do. Something isn't right, and I've got to stop it.

The moment the rectory comes into view, I notice an amber flicker of light inside. I barely make it to the archway when Logan's voice sounds at my ear.

"Close your eyes."

The way his *r*'s roll with his accent is absolutely the cutest thing I've ever heard. For a moment, I'm able to forget about my mom's sickness and the dark shadows in the castle.

"Close 'em, lass."

"You're crazy," I say.

"Aye," Logan says. "Crazy about you. Now close 'em."

My stomach does a flip and I close my eyes.

"Step right straight ahead, easy," he whispers. I do as he says. "Keep goin'."

The crackle of fire sounds in my ear, and a sweet scent permeates the usual old, wet stone smell.

"Keep goin'. Easy."

An impatient sigh escapes me, and I hear Logan's triumphant chuckle that he's truly gotten one over on me.

"Okay," he finally says. "Open your eyes."

Slowly, I do. My gaze moves over the once barren rectory, and my mouth drops open in surprise.

Candles — no fewer than twenty — are perched and flickering on every existing surface. A small peat fire burns in the hearth. And at our double window seat, where I always play, is a thick woolen plaid blanket, and a small table. On the table, there's a big vase of humongous pink flowers.

"So," Logan says softly beside me. "What do you think?"

"It's . . . I love it," I say, and turn to meet his gaze. Never in my life has anyone done anything remotely this romantic for me. "It's perfect."

Logan's silver eyes drop to my mouth, then slowly back up. "I've decided," he begins, his voice steady, a bit raspy, "that it's been well worth being a lost soul for almost two centuries." He comes close to me and traces his hand against my jaw. "If it means havin' you in the end, Ivy Calhoun."

"I can feel your touch against my face," I say, my voice quivering. "It's a faint tingle, but I feel it. It's . . . you." My heart is beating so hard, I'm sure it can be seen through my shirt.

"Aye," Logan answers, and I'm frozen in time. "'Tis me, Ivy."

In the golden-lit rectory we stand almost touching, looking at each other.

"I'm so verra glad to have met you," he whispers, and slowly, Logan dips his head toward me. He slants his mouth to mine and leans in, gently. My knees weaken, and my erratic heart skips a beat or two.

"*Is ann riut a bha mo dhùil a riamh,*" he says softly, moving the words against my lips. "*Mairidh mo ghaol gu siorraidh*, Ivy Calhoun," he whispers.

"What does that mean?" I manage to whisper back.

"I have waited for you my whole life," he says, his eyes searing into mine. "I'll love you forever."

"I love you, Logan Munro," I answer, my voice cracking. Then I lose myself in the sensation of his ghostly lips hovering over mine.

It's not quite a kiss, but it's the closest we can get. I breathe in the moment.

I'm being kissed by the sweetest, cutest soul. Ever.

And he loves me.

I'll worry about the fact that he's a ghost later.

Chapter 18

◦ THE RING ◦

I know now I'll never, ever be the same again. I'm in love with the spirit of a boy who lived almost two hundred years ago.

It doesn't make sense. Yet it makes perfect sense. Actually, there's no other sense but this one. Does that make sense? I'm laughing at myself, because to me, it does. It's all clear as a bell. Destiny. I now fully believe in it.

It was destiny that led Niall to my mom's emergency room.

And it was definitely destiny that led me to Glenmorrag, and to Logan Munro.

I have a purpose here. Not just to solve the frightening goings-on at the castle, or the mystery behind Logan's disappearance. But to know Logan.

After I play my violin for Logan in the rectory, I call Ethan and Amelia to update them. They feel it's not a coincidence that Elizabeth found the ring on the night of the elemental storm, and then changed personality. They think there's a very good chance that the ring is cursed. Possessed.

And we have to get it away from her.

Or at least off of her.

Logan agrees. He walks with me back into the castle, and he heads up to the third floor while I stop at my mom's room again. I peek inside the door.

And what I see scares me. My mother looks worse. Her cheeks are sunken. Her lips are pale. Niall is standing by the window, chewing his lip. Elizabeth is directly by her bed, sitting in a chair. She's touching that ring. I want to rush over there and yank it off of her, but doing that in front of Mom and Niall would only cause chaos. When she looks at me, the old woman's watery gaze turns dark.

I swallow a gasp.

"Niall," I whisper, feeling frantic. I wave him over. "I think Mom needs to go to the hospital."

And get away from Elizabeth, I add silently.

"I've already spoken to the physician about it," Niall whispers back. "He wants to give it a few more days."

"Don't worry so much, sweetie," Mom rasps, surprising me. I didn't know she was awake. "I trust my doctor. He can treat me just as easily here," she insists. "Besides, the hospital has more germs than anywhere else."

I study her, then sigh. "A few more days, Mom. But I want a progress report of your condition every single day. Then we'll see. Okay?"

"Okay, baby," she answers. "I'll get some sleep now."

I keep my eye on Elizabeth's ruby ring as I slowly shut the door.

Upstairs, my room's dark, all except the light from the lamp beside my bed. I pull the gray plaid bed curtains tight and crawl beneath the covers. I flip off the lamp, determined to get some rest, too.

"Good night, love. Sleep well," Logan's accent drifts from beyond my bedroom door where he stands guard all night.

In the darkness, I sigh. I feel so much better knowing he's there.

"Good night," I call back. "See you in the morning."

Under my pillow, my hand finds the two shards of yew Ethan gave me. One of them belongs to Logan, and I keep it for him. Soon, my eyes drift shut, but my mind continues to work furiously. How to get the ring from Elizabeth? Is the ring truly a way for the possessed Elizabeth to control malicious spirits? Is she using it to make Mom sick?

Why?

Around me, the house breathes, and I can hear it. Wind pierces the cracks in the stone and whines through the corridor. Unable to sleep, I flip on my lamp and finish reading the ghost story I'd checked out of the Glenmorrag library. Then I set it on the nightstand and flip out the light. Eventually, slumber overtakes me, and despite the odd sounds of the castle, I fall asleep. I've no idea how long I stay that way.

An agonizing scream rips through the night.

I bolt up in my bed, webs of confusion blocking my coherent thoughts. "Mom?" I say out loud. It's my immediate thought, my immediate concern. "Mom?" I yell. Logan's already by my side as I'm climbing out of bed.

"Shh," he says, trying to calm me with his voice, his presence. "What's the matter?"

"You didn't hear that scream?" I ask. Bewilderment flusters me. "It tore me out of my sleep. It's my mom, I'm sure of it. I'm not waiting another second to end this." I begin to scurry around the room, pulling on an oversized sweater to cover my pajamas.

"Whoa, whoa. Calm yourself. I heard nothin', Ivy," he says. "Are you sure you didna dream it?"

"No!" I say. "I heard a scream. And it wasn't a peacock." I find my All Stars and shove my sockless feet into them. "I'm going to check it out."

"No, wait," Logan says. "Hold on. No need for you to go tearin' through the castle and gettin' yourself all worked up. I'll go check on your mum. You stay here."

He's looking at me with a steady, calm gaze. "All right, then?" he asks.

I nod. "Okay. But hurry."

His gaze is still fully on mine as he disappears.

For lack of anything better to do, I pace. My mind races as unpleasant thoughts crowd inside of it. What if it is my mom? If it is, I'm not listening to another word from Niall or anyone else. I'll call 9-1-1. Or the UK version of it. I'll call for help. Period.

It's then that my door slams shut on its own. With my heart in my throat, I scan my room. My eyes light on the large picture window, and I stifle a scream with my hand over my mouth. The blood in my veins turns cold.

A face — Elizabeth's — is floating at the window. She stares back at me.

My heart is pounding viciously now, and as fast as it takes me to blink, the face disappears. Just as I run to the window, Logan appears.

"Your mum is sleeping peacefully, Ivy," he says, then frowns. "What is it?"

I land on the cushioned window seat with one knee, and press my hands against the glass as I stare out. Logan's words register in my head and relief washes over me that my mom is safe.

But there's something else now. As Logan moves next to me, I point to the courtyard below. The face now stares up at me from the body of a woman. Elizabeth.

"What is it?" Logan says.

"You don't see her?" I gasp. "She's down there, staring straight up here."

"I dunna see her, Ivy. Who is it?" he asks.

"It's Elizabeth," I respond.

Logan moves closer, his gaze searching below. "I see nothing but an empty courtyard."

"Why can't you see her?" I demand fiercely, and tap the glass. "She's right there!"

"I dunna know," Logan responds. "Ivy, calm down. Are you sure you see —"

"Yes!" My eyes won't leave the image of Elizabeth below. But now she looks . . . different. Black, gaping orbs that are her eyes and mouth stare up at me, and although she doesn't speak and that strange mouth doesn't move, she beckons me. Then she turns her ring on her finger and begins to walk away.

"She wants me to follow her," I say, and just that fast I'm halfway to the door. "I'm going to get that ring."

"Ivy, wait!" Logan yells. He's on my heels and then beside me. He moves ahead of me, making me stop, and looms over me. "You dunna do anythin' without me checkin' it out first, aye?"

"Okay," I answer, then take off again. I fly down the staircase as quietly as I can, taking two at a time, and all but skid across the great hall. Gently, I open the door and race out into a mist-shrouded night. Logan's right by my side, though, and I feel safe.

I catch sight of the figure up ahead and come to a stop.

"You see her?" Logan asks.

"Yes," I answer. "She's standing right beside that old twisted tree."

"Ivy," he says slowly. "That's the rowan."

My heart leaps.

"Did you bring your yew sliver?" he asks.

Oh, shoot. "No."

Logan mutters what must be a Gaelic curse word.

"She's pointing at me, Logan," I say. "And she's pointing at the rowan tree."

"Och," Logan mutters, frustrated. "Why canna I see her?"

"She wants only me," I answer, shivering. "And she doesn't see you. She wants to show me something."

The wind picks up, blowing thin wisps of mist. I move slowly toward Elizabeth. Logan stays by my side.

She seems surreal, almost blending in with the mist swirling around her bare feet. The wind blows fiercely now, yet the rhythmic flow of her nightgown reflects a different, gentler breeze. And still, those dark orbs stare blankly at me. Not at me, yet beckoning me. I should be frightened, but I'm not.

Hesitantly, I move closer. Closer, still, until I'm nearly at the tree.

"What is it you want?" I demand.

She's pointing to a nondescript clump of ivy and moss at the base of the rowan tree. As I walk toward it, she disappears.

Dropping to my knees, I ignore the frigid wind biting through my sweater and pajama pants, and pull back the vines. I gasp.

"It's a door," Logan says.

"Did you know this was here?" I ask without looking at him. "It looks like it's been here a long time."

"I had no idea," Logan admits.

With my palm, I graze the old door, then the rusty iron padlock hanging from it. "The wood's all rotted," I say, then without hesitation, I stand, share a look with Logan, and kick the door. The aged wood smashes like smoked kindling. "There's something down there," I say, peering into the shadowy hole.

"Ivy, be careful," Logan warns. "Dunna get so close."

I give Logan a long look. "I'm going to get that ring off of her if I have to hold her down and yank it off. It has to be behind all of this," I plead. "And it might be behind what happened to you as well."

It's then that, all at once, I feel a pair of hands on my back. I'm shoved — hard — and before I even have a chance to scream, I've lost my balance. I'm falling straight into the gaping mouth of the hole.

I find my voice and yell as I tumble down, down, into the shadows.

I land hard on my back, and my head smacks against the rough surface. My body feels light, and everything around me begins to darken. Elizabeth leans over me, and frigid puffs of white escape her mouth and swirl over my face with each of her ragged breaths.

Logan's frantic cries reach me, just before a heavy pitch blanket smothers me and pulls me into a shroud of darkness.

Chapter 19

⁓ TRAPPED ⁓

"*I*vy! Answer me, please — Ivy!"

Logan's words, although muffled and far away, reach my ears. Opening my eyes, I focus on the very first thing I see.

Logan's handsome, fretful face. His brows are dark slashes above his silver eyes.

"Can you move at all?" he asks. He starts to touch me and draws back, clearly remembering he can't, really. "Ivy, answer me, can you move your arms? Your legs? Och, gell, I'm sae bloody useless!" His voice is harsh, angry, worried.

"It's okay, it's okay," I respond, and slowly push myself up onto my elbows. It's cold. Moonlight streams in from high above, illuminating Logan's strong features. When I sit all the way up, Logan's eyes close briefly, and he mutters something I can't hear.

"Can you stand?" he asks. His voice sounds pained.

"I'll try," I say, and with ease I push up to my feet and stand. Logan's worried expression tears at me. "I'm fine, Logan," I assure him gently. "Honest." I move my arms and legs. "Nothing broken."

Relief eases the lines of concern on his face. "Thank God," he says, then runs his knuckles close to my jaw, his gaze softening. "You scared me terribly, lass."

"It was Elizabeth," I say, suddenly remembering the moments before the fall. "She pushed me, Logan."

Logan's brows furrow as he frowns. "Ivy," he says with caution. "No one was there, save you and I."

Confusion makes my head spin. "But I felt a pair of hands push against my back when I fell," I say. "I saw her face, Logan. Saw it clear as day. She's the one who shoved me into the freezer, too. I'm sure of it." I shake my head. "It's that ruby ring. It's . . . possessed her. And she's making bad things happen with it. Including making my mom sick."

" 'Twill be all right," he reassures me. "But we have to find a way out of *here* first."

He's right. I search the small chamber I'd fallen into.

Shadows reach from the walls as the moon passes in and out of the clouds. In the distance, the sea crashes against the rocky base of Glenmorrag. With the scant light of the moon, I notice dust-laden wooden shelves lining the walls, sagging with the weight of jars filled with . . . something. A thick blanket of cobwebs covers other items, and the webs and dust are so thick I can't even tell what they are.

"This must've belonged to the old vicar," Logan says. "'Tis a food cellar."

"Then we're below the rectory," I say.

"Aye."

My fingers brush the binding of a leather-bound book, completely cleaned and webless. I slowly retrieve it and hold it out for Logan to see. "Look."

Walking toward the one shaft of moonlight in the dank chamber, I open the book and flip through the pages.

"It's a . . . book of spells," I say, and lean the leather-bound volume toward the small shaft of light illuminating the tomb. "There're spells for all sorts of stuff in here." I continue to read. "Commanding the dead." I flip the page. "Choking with rowan," I say, and shake my head. That must have been what was choking me that night.

"I remember," Logan says suddenly. "The ring."

I look up at him, confused. "What do you mean?"

"The ring commands the wearer," Logan explains, his eyes growing wide. "And the wearer uses the book of spells to command the spirits, make things happen." For a moment, he closes his eyes, then again looks at me. "I remember it now. My uncle Patrick . . . the ruby ring was a Munro relic, handed down through generations. But it was rumored to be cursed. Patrick didn't care. He was so proud to have found it, buried in the Munro keep. 'Twas there for centuries, hidden. I was right there when he placed it on his finger for the first time. Everything after that . . . changed." Logan glances at the tome. "I remember that book. He kept it in his croft, beside his bed. Wouldna let anyone get near it."

"But you got near it?"

Logan nods. "Aye."

"And then he killed you?" I ask.

"I dunna remember that part," he answers, and shakes his head. "I'm sorry."

I sigh. I'd give anything to comfort him more. "It's okay." I feel we're getting close, though. Close to some answers. I look back down at the book, and flip to a new page. There's a spell called Veil of the Living.

"I wish I could read these spells," Logan says, sounding frustrated. "Maybe then I could piece everything together. Can you read one to me, Ivy?"

"'Veil of the Living,'" I say, reading. "''Tis once you walk with a beating heart, now you'll drift as mist, forevermore.'" This is followed by a long string of Gaelic words, which I try to pronounce best I can.

When I look up at Logan, something is very wrong.

"You're fading, Logan," I say, growing panicked.

Logan glances down at himself, then back to me. He says nothing.

"Oh, you're almost see-through!" I cry, wanting to touch him, to grab on to him. "What's going on?"

"Ivy," he says calmly, but I'm still jumping around, trying to make the fading stop. "Ivy, shhh," he whispers. "It willna help."

"What won't help?" I say, bewildered. "Why not?"

"Because you just read the incantation that takes me out of this limbo," he answers, looking around, then at me. "I . . . canna stop it, Ivy."

Pain and terror grip my throat and squeeze. "No, Logan!" I say vehemently. "*No!*" I start flipping through the book like crazy. "Maybe there's a spell in here to reverse things." My eyes scan the pages. "There's got to be something!"

"Ivy, please, lass."

I look up and move closer to Logan and clench my fists. "You . . . can't go!" Tears sting my eyes.

Logan glances down at his vanishing form again. He's now nearly transparent. "Ivy, listen to me," he says frantically, his voice fading. "I feel myself slipping, and I'm sorry, lass. I didna expect this," he says, searching my eyes now. "I didna expect you."

"I want to go with you," I say quietly.

Mere inches separate us, and Logan's head is bent toward mine. "You listen to me, Ivy Calhoun. You canna remain here in this damp, moldy old tomb. You have to escape and tell the truth of that bloody ring, and get it away from Elizabeth. You have to destroy it. And the book of spells wi' it. As fast as you can."

My mind, my body is frozen. I can't believe what's happening. I can do little more than stare at Logan.

"Ivy! Hear me, gell! You have to do this, do you understand me? Look at me!"

Slowly, my eyes focus on Logan's fading, somber silver gaze. I nod.

"Promise me, Ivy, that you will do everything you can to escape this place. Promise me!"

"I promise," I say quietly, tears falling. "I promise."

"Thank you," he says, just as quiet.

"Feumaidh mi do leigeil as," he whispers against me. "I have tae let you go."

A cry rips at my throat.

"Fuirichidh mi riut," he says, his voice breaking. "I will wait for you."

Tears roll down my cheeks, unchecked. I'm losing Logan now, and sadness overwhelms me. I start to shake as I cry.

Logan's lips graze ever so close to mine, causing a tingle much softer than before, yet the sensation sinks straight to my soul. He's fading fast, I can feel it. I open my eyes and look at him. "Logan?"

"Mairidh mo ghaol gu siorraidh, Ivy Calhoun," he says, and I already know that means *I'll love you forever.*

"Forevermore," I say in return, and graze his cheek with my fingertip. "I'll love you always, Logan Munro."

A sad, somber smile touches his lips. Before he fades fully he says one last thing. *"Bi mi còmhla riut gu brath."* His eyes remain on mine. "I will always be with you."

Then he vanishes completely.

"No!" I yell, tears streaming down my face. "Come back!" The cold air freezes the tears against my skin, and I scan the small room. "Logan, come back." I wait a few moments, my heart beating out of control. "Logan?" I say, hoping a part of him still remains. My ears strain for even the slightest of sounds. A feeling. A sensation.

Nothing. Everything is completely still, inaudibly silent.

Inside, I'm dying. Tears scald the back of my eyelids and spill out. How did I grow to love someone — a ghost — in such a short time? I've had crushes before, back in Charleston. Nothing of substance.

This, with Logan? It's real. And it hurts.

I stand there, in the shadows of a long-forgotten vicar's pantry, wrap my arms around myself, and sob. Heart-wrenching cries feel as though they're being ripped from my chest. Time passes in such a way that I don't even know how long I stand there. It's not until the damp chill from being underground begins to seep through my sweater that I stop. Drying my eyes with my sleeves, I take a deep breath in and let it out slowly.

Logan's gone. I don't feel him anymore. Somehow, by reading aloud that ancient spell, I freed his spirit.

He's finally with his mother, as it should be.

Like my mother needs me.

I need to get out of here.

Pushing aside my grief, I search the darkened chamber for a way to escape. There, hidden in the recesses of shadow, I find a small door. There is no bolt or lock, so with the palm of my hand, I push against the aged wood. Slowly, it creaks open, and a cold, shadowy tunnel stretches before me. Stale, cold air wafts toward me on an icy draft. Knocking cobwebs from above, I follow the path to a narrow flight of uneven stone steps. I glance behind me, for what reason I don't know, and then with caution, I begin to climb. Thirteen steps in all. At the top, another door, smaller, sturdier, and more modern than the ones below. The lock on it is shiny silver. The wood is far from rotten. I bang my fist on it.

"Hey!" I holler. "Can anyone hear me?" I bang some more. "Hello! Is anyone there?"

I wait, listen. A draft of air seeps from around the door and brushes my cheek. But I hear no sounds at all from behind the door. I can only assume it's somewhere inside the castle, judging from the length of the tunnel. But I have no idea where.

I pound on the door, shouting and calling out for at least an hour. My throat starts to burn and my voice grows hoarse. It's no use. No one can hear me. No one's coming.

I have to find another way out.

Moving back down the stone steps, I follow the damp, chilly tunnel back to the food cellar. Standing beneath the hole I fell through, I stare up into the moonlight. Then I run my hands over the walls. I try to find footing with the toe of my shoe, but it keeps slipping. The more I try, the more frustrated I become. It's impossible! The walls are way too smooth. "Hey!" I yell, hoping someone will hear me. "Hello?"

My voice becomes crackly and ineffective, and I'm exhausted. I'm reminded of being trapped in the freezer. I sit, right below the hole above me, and simply . . . breathe. Weariness overcomes me, and I rest my forehead against my knees. My mind wanders.

Maybe this is my destiny? Am I supposed to die here?

I shiver. What if I'm never found? If I die right here, in the food cellar, will I then be with Logan? I don't know if I want that, though. I still want to live. Logan would want that for me, too. I know he would.

If only he were here with me now. . . .

Chapter 20

✑ SACRED PROMISES ✑

Ivy!

My body bolts up, my heart pounding against my ribs. "Logan?" I whisper.

I glance around, rub my eyes, stretch my stiff back and legs. I must have dozed off a little, sitting there in a daze.

And it suddenly all comes rushing back, flooding my memory like torrential rain.

Logan. The ring. Elizabeth. The book of spells.

Faint, hazy early-dawn light seeps down from the hole above. I clear my dry throat and holler. "Hey! Is anybody out there? Hello?"

Footsteps crunch against gravel, grow closer. "Hello!" I yell. "I'm down here!"

I pray it's not Elizabeth.

"Ivy? What on earth are you down there for?" Niall's face stares down at me from above. "Are you hurt?"

"Niall! I can't get out."

He peers down and glances about. "What's down there?"

"I think it's the vicar's old food cellar," I answer. "Can you help me? Please?"

"Of course I can," he answers. "I'll be right back," he says, and disappears from the hole.

Suddenly, I'm anxious — dying to get out of the dark, dingy cellar. I clutch the book of spells to my chest and wait.

I've got work to do.

Luckily, I don't have to wait long. The sound of a tractor's engine grows close, then idles.

"Step aside, lass," Niall says, emerging over the hole again. "I'm goin' tae drop this rope down." He does, and the heavy rope hits the cellar floor with a thud. "There's a loop at the end, see?" he says.

"Yes, I see," I answer.

"Good. Wind your leg 'round the rope, then stick your foot in the loop. And then hold on."

"Okay," I respond, tucking the book into the waist of

my pajama pants. Then I do as Niall asks. "I'm ready," I yell up.

"Hold on, gell," Niall hollers down. "I'm goin' tae let the tractor pull you most of the way up, then I'll help you." He moves away from the hole once more, and I hear as he shifts the tractor into first gear.

With a jerk, I start to rise from the cellar. As I grow close to the hole, I wonder if Niall's going to stop. Then he does, and his head appears once more. "Okay, lass, I'll pull you the rest of the way. When you clear the top, grab on to the ledge, all right?"

"Okay," I say, a little breathless.

Niall begins to pull, and within seconds my head clears. I grip the edge of the rotted door and pull myself over. Quickly, I roll from the hole and stand. I take a deep, cleansing breath, shaky and relieved.

"Thank you, Niall," I say, feeling choked up at the sight of him. I never thought I'd be so grateful toward my stepdad. I withdraw the book, which was beginning to slip down my pants leg.

"What happened tae you, Ivy?" he asks. "You're in your sleep clothes. Down there all night, were you?"

"Yes," I answer. "I . . . fell."

Niall shakes his head. "Let's get you inside before you catch your death."

Niall drapes his jacket over my shoulders and then walks with me. Mist slips over the ground, so thick I can't even see my feet as we hurry toward the front doors.

I stumble inside — and nearly straight into Elizabeth. I pull up short, breathless. My skin tingles with fear, adrenaline. Our gazes are locked.

A slow smile stretches across her wrinkled face. Then her face shifts, blurs, changes . . . into another. I blink, and a frightening laugh emerges from her throat.

The ring. I have to get it. And without another thought, I reach down, grab the old woman's bony hand, and yank that ring off her finger.

Elizabeth wails as though I'm killing her.

"Grandmother? What's the matter with you?" Niall asks.

I don't spare another second. I shove past Elizabeth and race to the staircase. At once, the air around me grows icy cold, and my breath billows out before me in white puffs. Doors begin to rattle, open and slam shut, and I run faster. A chilling laughter accompanies me all the way to the second floor.

The moment I hit the second-floor landing, the whispers begin.

"Niall!" I shout, running up the shadowy corridor that seems to breathe. It crowds me, and I run faster. Doors are rattling on their hinges, and the whispers grow louder, condensed. Fear pulls at me, and an overwhelming sense of panic engulfs me. "Niall!" I cry again, my voice trembling. At my mother's door, just as I grab the handle, it opens. Niall is right behind me, and he follows me into my mother's room.

"Aye, Ivy?" he says, worry furrowing his brows. "What's wrong wi' you, pullin' on Gran like you did? Now tell me how you ended up —"

I run straight past him and into the chamber. I find my mom, asleep, but she doesn't awaken. Just lies there, still as death.

"Mom," I say, and hurry to her. I press my face against her shoulder, tears falling down my cheek. "Mom," I repeat, unable to say anything else. She's not answering.

"Ivy! What's wrong wi' you?" Niall hollers.

I don't stick around to answer. The ring and the book have to be destroyed. Now. I take off running to my room.

"Ivy!"

I don't stop.

I fly into my room, throw on jeans and a hoodie, pull a hat over my head, and shove the ring in my pocket. With the book of spells tucked inside my down coat, I grab my cell, think twice, and grab the shards of yew tree from under my pillow. I run, and I don't stop until I'm out of the castle. The moment I'm outside, I call Emma. Fortunately, we have the next two days off of school thanks to faculty conferences.

"Em, I need you now!" I say frantically into the phone. "Can you get a ride?"

"Aye, my mum will take me — Ivy, what's wrong?"

"Meet me at the seawall when you get here. I've got the ring. Hurry!"

"Och, I'm hurryin'!"

Then I call Amelia. She answers on the second ring.

"Amelia!" I say. A thick haze of mist rolls in from the sea, and the cold freezes the air in my lungs. "I've got the ring, and we found a book of spells. I was pushed into an old vicar's cellar, and Logan's gone, and —"

"Honey, hold on!" Amelia says. "Slow down. You've got the ring?"

"Yes!"

"Logan's gone? Are you sure?" she asks. Her voice is laced with urgency.

A sob cracks my throat. "Yes, I'm sure."

"Oh, sweetie," Amelia says.

"I don't know what to do," I say, and panic grabs me. "What . . . do I do?"

"Okay, okay, everything's going to be all right," Amelia says soothingly. "Sit tight. I'll call you right back, you understand?"

"I understand," I say, and Amelia hangs up the phone.

It seems like I pace the seawall for an hour before Emma shows up. Her mom drops her off and all I see are wild ginger curls flying in the wind as Em races toward me. She skids to a halt. Her face is drawn in worry.

"What's wrong? You've got the ring?" She looks around. "Where's Logan?"

I shake my head. "He's . . . gone, Em." I show her the book, and pull the ring from my pocket. "The moment we found this book in the cellar, and I read the Veil of the Living spell, he started to disappear." Tears scorch my eyes again.

"Whoa, what's with the cellar?" she asks.

As fast as I can, I tell Emma about getting pushed into the vicar's cellar, finding the book, snatching the ring off Elizabeth, and seeing my mom.

For once, Emma's speechless, and just reaches out to hug me. I do feel better having her support.

My cell rings, and I answer. "Amelia?"

"Nay, 'tis Ethan," the voice says. "Do exactly as I say, aye?"

"Okay," I answer.

"Do you have your yew sliver?" he asks.

"I do, yes," I answer.

"Good girl. Now take the ring and the book down by the sea," Ethan orders. "Hurry. And Amelia wants tae know if you're alone."

"No, Emma's with me."

"Make sure she has her yew as well."

I hand Emma the second sliver of yew.

We take the path that leads down to the shore. Once there, I could swear the ring is burning a hole in my fist. I want it gone.

Forever.

"Amelia says for me to be on speakerphone," Ethan says, and I do the same at my end so that Emma can hear him, too. "Right. The ring and book cannot be touching anything live," he continues. "Find a pile of dried seaweed. Place it on a rock."

"Aye!" Emma says. She retrieves a bunch of dried seaweed from the shore, and heaps it all on a big flat rock nearby.

"Place the book atop the seaweed," Ethan instructs. "And the ring atop the book."

I follow each step. I set the book in the center of the seaweed, and the ruby ring atop the closed book. It's not touching anything but the weed, on top of a rock. Nothing living.

"Okay, it's done," I yell over the wind and surf. "Now what?"

" 'Tis a verse in Gaelic," Ethan says. "You'll have tae try and repeat it exactly as me, word for word. Can you do that, Ivy?"

"Yes," I say, breathless. I remember how I read the spell in Gaelic last night — how it worked a little too well. "I can."

Ethan recites the incantation, and word by word, I repeat it. The language sounds strange on my tongue, yet . . . right. I remember all the words Logan spoke to me last night, and knowing that I'm speaking his language makes me feel strong and safe.

As I speak, the seaweed begins to smolder, then smoke. My voice grows louder, the ancient language sounds natural on my tongue, and a gale wind kicks up. It's so fierce that I have to grab on to Emma and hold on.

Finally, Ethan finishes the incantation — I recite the last word and wait a heartbeat. There's a loud *boom* and then everything on the rock — the seaweed, the book, and the ring — erupts into a sonic explosion that throws me and Em backward. I hit the sand on my side, the air knocked from my lungs. As I push myself up, I see smoke. It rises from the rock.

After a few moments, the smoke clears. The seaweed, the book, the ring — all gone. Emma and I share a long, understanding look.

"Ivy?" Ethan says harshly on the phone. "Lass, are you two all right?"

"Yes," I call out, and breathe a sigh of relief. "The ring and book have disappeared."

"Och, well done, then," Ethan says. "Well done."

"Thank you, Ethan," I say. "So much."

"You'll be fine, lass," he offers. "I vow it. Now my wife wants a word with you."

"Hey." Amelia comes on the line. "You guys okay?"

I look again at Emma, and her wild crazy hair swirling all around her face. I'm so happy she's all right. We exchange a quick hug. "Yeah," I answer. "We're fine."

"You will be, Ivy," Amelia echoes her husband's words. "I promise."

I doubt it, but it's all for the best. The ring is destroyed. No one else can be hurt. But . . .

"My mom," I say frantically, jumping up. "Amelia, I'll call you later. I'm going to check on Mom."

"Okay, hon," she says. "I'll be here."

Emma and I hurry up the path, back to the seawall and across the courtyard. Inside, we both rush upstairs. I glance at Emma in the hall. "Wait here," I say. "Just in case."

"Okay," she agrees.

I go straight into my mom's room.

Mom is sitting up in bed, looking straight at me. Her eyes are clear and her cheeks have color in them. "There's my girl!" Mom says.

"Are you feeling better?" I ask, hurrying over to her. "I've been worried sick."

Mom hugs me. "I do feel better now," she says. "Niall has taken good care of me."

I glance around. "Where is he? And Elizabeth?" I ask.

Mom sighs. "Elizabeth started feeling ill, so he's called the physician to take a look at her."

I study Mom. The dark circles that had been under her eyes have already faded. Her bright blue gaze sparkles.

"They said I had a respiratory infection," she explains. "Not bad enough to be admitted to the hospital."

"I'm so glad!"

"Me too. It's like it's been . . . lifted off of me." She grins. "Except I think I could eat a cow. Well, a burger. With lettuce, tomato, onion, pickles, mayo, mustard, and ketchup. Oh, and French fries!" She rubs her belly. "I'm eating for two now, remember?"

Tears fill my eyes. I am so relieved. All I want is for my mom and the baby to be all right.

"I'm so happy for you," I say, and hug her. "And I'm sorry if I've been a snotty brat since moving here," I blurt out. "Actually, since you and Niall got married." I shrug.

"Maybe I was a little jealous. Like he was taking my mom away."

"Oh, sweetie," Mom says, and strokes my cheek. "That could never happen." She smiles. "You'll always be my baby."

I pat her belly. "I'll have to share now," I say. "But I'm okay with it. I really am. I'm just happy you're better."

"Me too, baby," she says. "You know nurses make the worst patients anyway."

I grin, kiss her cheek, and leave my mom to rest.

Emma and I walk to my room. "Thanks for getting over here so fast," I say, and flop on my bed. I look at her. "Thanks for everything."

Emma flops down beside me. We both stare at the ceiling.

" 'Twas destiny, Ivy," she answers. "You movin' here. Us meetin'. Knowin' Serrus. His kin being Logan's kin." She turns her head toward me, and I push a wad of red curls out of the way so I can see her face. She grins.

"So are you and Serrus . . . ?" I ask, feeling hopeful for my friend.

She nods, beaming. "He kissed me the other day. When he was dropping me off at home. I guess we're dating now?"

"I'm excited for you," I tell Emma, meaning it. I squeeze her hand, but a lump rises in my throat when I think about the boy I loved — and lost.

Emma must see my expression change, because she squeezes my hand back.

"Trust the Munros," she advises softly. "When they say 'twill be all right . . ." She smiles, her eyes crinkling. ". . . it for a certainty will be."

Chapter 21

A little while later, Emma's mom picks her up. I wave good-bye from the front steps, then close the heavy doors of Glenmorrag Castle. But just as I'm doing so, there's a knock on the door — the physician has arrived. I let him in. He's tall and bespectacled, and he's carrying a black leather doctor's bag.

"Dr. MacEwan, you're here," Niall says, appearing behind me. "Grandmother's feeling a bit winded today," he adds. "Follow me."

Niall glances briefly at me, and leads the doctor to Elizabeth's first-floor room. I follow, almost afraid of what I'll find. Will Elizabeth still be evil? Will she remember?

What I find when I peek in is a frail, sobbing old woman, lying in bed.

She sees me walk in. "Oh, Ivy," she says through her tears. "I'm ever so sorry, lass. Come here."

I blink. *Does* she remember? Slowly, I walk toward her.

"For what?" I ask.

"Well, for being a mean old goat, for one," she says. Her voice is different. Her eyes are softer. Everything about her says sweet little old granny.

I'm in shock. Was the magic truly that dark, black, and fast?

"It's okay, Lady Elizabeth," I say gently. "Really."

"Please," she begs. "Gran. 'Tis what my boy here calls me."

Niall smiles at me, and nods.

"Sure thing, Gran," I say.

Niall pats his grandmother's arm and we leave her in the physician's care.

In the hall, Niall turns to me and gives a winsome smile. The lines that fan out at the corners of his eyes seem a little deeper this morning, though. "I'm . . . sorry, for everything, Ivy," he begins. "You know, for no' trying

to . . . understand things a bit better. With you," he clarifies. "I know it's been hard on you since your mother and
I have wed. I hope things — we — can get to know each
other a wee bit better?"

I return the smile, and it comes easy. "I'd like that,
Niall," I say.

In his eyes I see honesty, sincerity, and I'm again so
glad that he's innocent in everything involving the ring.
"I never once fancied the thought tae take the place of
your da," he says solemnly. "But if you need a fatherly figure to talk to, ever . . ." He dips his head in a frank nod.
"You come to me. Anytime. And I'm sorry it took sae
long tae tell you as much."

I see Niall in a whole new light, and it fills me with
a sense of peace I haven't had in a long time. "Thanks,
Niall. I appreciate that. And I'm sorry if I've been a teen-
aged brat." I smile. "I'll work on that."

A boyish grin makes him look years younger. "You've
no' been a brat, Ivy," he says. "You're a fine young lass with
an extraordinary gift." He nods. "I'm glad we're family now."

And I am, too. I climb the stairs with Niall, and he
parts at the second floor to go see about my mom. I head
to my room, alone.

A heavy feeling settles over me as I walk up to the third floor. Exhaustion pulls at me, and something else. Something much weightier than sleep deprivation. It's a pressure, building inside of my chest, and by the time I make it to my room, I kick my shoes off and fall into bed. My body wants to sleep, but my mind races to counteract it. So much has happened, and in a short amount of time.

It's now all starting to sink in. Really, really sink in.

That pressure in my chest tightens, and my throat begins to burn. Tears break through and stream down my cheek and onto my pillow.

"Logan?" I whisper out loud. I dry my cheek with my sleeve. "Are you there?"

Straining my ears, I stare into the dim haze of the barely there light of my room. Everything is still, the shadows are silent, and the only sound I hear is the wind pushing through the cracks of the old stone walls. I try again.

"Logan?"

I wait. Seconds go by. My chest tightens, and my eyes drift shut.

"I can't feel you anymore. . . ."

I cry myself to sleep, the void of Logan's absence a hollow, aching hole in my gut, a pain that won't ease up.

I hope that, in my dreams, Logan will be there, smiling, laughing, urging me to play my strings. Eagerly, he sits, listens, watches me. In my dreams, I will hear his Gaelic endearments, that rich, raspy accented voice.

Mairidh mo ghaol gu siorraidh. . . .

I'll love you forever. . . .

Finally, I slip into slumber, and I drift, until the tears stop flowing and I'm resting, peaceful, still as the air around me.

Ivy . . .

I bolt up in my bed. "Logan?" I say out loud. The room is shrouded in darkness, and I've no idea how long I've been asleep. Wasn't my name just called? Hadn't that been the sound that woke me up? Or am I losing my mind?

Lying back, I stare at the canopy of gray plaid above me, and my thoughts are full force on Logan. In the darkness, I breathe and recall his image to my mind. It comes easy, as I knew it would.

I would've loved to know more about him. Everything about him — before his death, and after. At least we'd had some time together, I tell myself. We spoke of likes and dreams, of dislikes, and we walked Glenmorrag's lands until I knew every single rock and tree. I Googled things I thought he'd like on my laptop and watched as his eyes widened in amazement at cars, planes, music videos on YouTube. I'll cherish those times forever. I wish we hadn't been so preoccupied with the sleuthing and the dark force that was tormenting me.

Play for me. . . .

I get out of bed, press the violin against my chin, and begin to play. For me, and for Logan, and the memory of us.

The next day, the weather has turned downright wintry. You can't go outside with less than several layers, coat, boots, hat, scarf, gloves. Not too much of a problem as I've grown accustomed to the cold now and sort of like it. It's crisp, clean, and makes my lungs feel good. Mom is doing better but still resting, as is Elizabeth. I can't believe this dark spirit has lifted from us at last but I feel it — the peace and calm within the walls of the castle. If only Logan were here to enjoy it with me.

I take a long walk by the cliffs and even down the beach. The wind nearly tears my skin off, it's so frigid, but I love the view. For as brutal as it can be, it's majestic at the same time. As I'm headed back, I run into Ian, and we walk the rest of the way together. I tell him about Logan — how I accidentally read his spell out loud, and he disappeared. Ian understands. He listens.

As Ian and I cross the bailey to the courtyard, the ever-present gray gloom still lingers over Glenmorrag. The trees are stark and desolate, with spindly limbs that reach out like bony dead fingers. The only color notice-able is the blue of the peacocks. I watch them now, hovering together by the stone wall separating the bailey from the inner courtyard. The indigo stands in severe con-trast to the black-and-white surroundings. It's almost . . . comforting.

"Here you go, then," Ian says, and waves me on to the front door. "I'll see you later, lass." His eyes meet mine and soften. "If you want someone tae talk to, I'll be 'round."

I smile. "Thanks, Ian."

With a single nod, he disappears around the side of the courtyard.

Voices reach my ears, and I pause on the steps. When

I turn, I find Emma, Cam and Derek, and Serrus trotting across the grounds toward me. I wave to them, feeling my spirits lift.

"Hey, guys!" I call. "What's up?" My eyes drift to Serrus, whose Munro looks are almost painful to see. He drapes an arm around me.

"We thought you might like some company," he says in his Highland brogue. "We're a fun lot." He throws his head toward the others. "Well, mostly me."

We all laugh, and I invite them in for some of Jonas's tea and shortbread. It is so comforting to have friends. Especially Emma. We've bonded in ways my girlfriends back home and I just didn't. She's special. She believed in Logan. She and Serrus feel like my last connection to him. Ethan, Amelia, and the rest of the Munros do, too, but I haven't been in touch with them since Emma and I destroyed the ring and the spell book.

The weekend passes quickly once my friends are around, and soon it's Wednesday. School drags, and my thoughts are elsewhere. But it's a joy to see Mom in the car with Niall, come to pick me up at the end of the day. She's finally up and about.

"Hey," Mom says, perky as ever. "How was school?"

I buckle my seat belt and peer at her as Niall starts off down the school's drive. She seems . . . extra perky. Extra glowy.

"Fine," I answer, studying her closely. Something's up. Mom's looking guilty. Proudly so.

Then I remember. Today she and Niall went to the doctor to have an ultrasound.

Mom's face is full of excitement. She looks as though she's about to burst.

"Okay, Mom," I say. "I can't wait another second. Do I have a sister or a brother?"

Mom glances at Niall, who grins ear to ear. Then she looks at me and gives a firm nod. "Yes."

"Well, which is it?" I ask, looking between her and Niall, thinking they've lost it. They both burst out laughing.

"Maybe one of each," Mom announces.

It takes me a second for her comment to register. My eyes stretch wide. "Twins?"

Mom laughs again. "Can you believe it? Two wee MacAllisters!"

Niall's face is glowing just as brightly as Mom's. I can't help but laugh, too. "Man, you guys are going to be super busy," I say. "Congratulations."

"Niall has a surprise for you, too," Mom says, and slides her husband a sly look. "Sweetheart?"

Niall glances at me through the rearview mirror. "I thought you might like a more comfortable place to play your music," he says, smiling. "So I'm having the rectory remodeled for you." He pauses. "If you'd like."

Surprise shakes me. "Of course I'd like!" I say excitedly. "Wow, I don't know what to say." I glance at Mom, who is still grinning ear to ear. "Thanks, Niall. That means a lot to me."

He nods. "I know it does, Ivy. And I'm happy tae do it."

I sit back and watch the scenery flash by. Still bleak, still cold as anything, but different now. Maybe because I'm a little different now? Scotland has definitely grown on me, as has my stepfather. And not just because he's remodeling the rectory for me. Ever since that horrible day, when I escaped the cellar, Niall and I have seemed closer. I suppose it will continue to get even better as time passes.

As for Elizabeth — Gran — she's also up and about when we get home, wearing a robe, her fingers bare without that awful ring. She greets me warmly and seems thrilled when Mom and Niall share with her their news about the twins. I know Mom has noticed the change in Elizabeth, too, and has chalked it up to the MacAllister matriarch finally coming around to her new American family. I haven't told Mom or Niall anything about the ring, and the curse, and the Gaelic incantation that broke the spell. Gran herself seems to have very little memory of the time she was possessed — she just recalls not being very nice to me. As far as I'm concerned, that's all she needs to know.

Nightfall is hard for me. It's when the memories of Logan come thick and fast. I'm so used to Logan being right outside my door, my own personal watchman. At times, I hear his voice so clearly in my head, I think I've heard it for real. I call his name. He never answers.

I wonder if, in time, he'll be easier to think of without my chest hurting so much. For now, I'll have to learn to live with the pain.

Early Sunday morning, a horn blasting outside my window wakes me. I get out of bed and draw back the drapes.

Just beyond the courtyard, I see a big work truck — rather, a lorry, as they call them here in Scotland. I feel a shiver of excitement. Today the restorations on the rectory begin, and they're starting by digging up the old floor — or what's left of it. I want to watch, so I hurry and pull on my favorite holey jeans, a striped long-sleeved T-shirt, and a snap-up cotton shirt over that. Layers, I've learned, keep me warmer in the frigid winter Highlands. After yanking on socks and boots, I brush my teeth and fly down the stairs. Niall is already at the hall closet, my wool coat and hat in hand.

He grins. "Come on, then."

"I'm coming, too," my mom says, making her way from the kitchen. She has on her bright pink hat and matching scarf. She's wearing a long-sleeved T-shirt that says *Babies*, with an arrow pointing down at her belly. It's ridiculous and cheesy, but I can't begrudge Mom anything now. She grins at me, and I shake my head, take my hat and coat from Niall, and start out the door.

I lead the way down the gravel path to the rectory, the wind fierce at my back. Niall and Mom are behind me a ways, and I can hear their feet crunching as they walk. Ahead, the workers have already started loading their equipment inside the ruins. I find a place that has a decent view into the main chamber of the rectory, lean against a tree, and watch. Niall and Mom join me.

We watch for about half an hour as the workers bring equipment inside, rattle around in there. I'm dying of curiosity but Niall has said it might not be safe to go in. He whispers to me, so Mom won't hear, that he doesn't want me falling into any other holes. I can understand.

It's freezing out and Mom can't stand the cold anymore. "Okay, guys," she says, rubbing her arms through her insulated down jacket. "Hungry. Thirsty. Cold. I'm done." Her nose is cherry red as she glances from me to Niall. "So I'm going inside. Grilled cheese. Hot chocolate. Fireplace. Join me?"

Niall kisses Mom's cheek. "I'll be along in a few, love. I wouldn't mind watching with Ivy for a little longer."

Mom smiles at me, and I know it's because she is beyond happy that Niall and I have finally connected. "Okay," she says, and starts up the path toward the castle. "I'll save you guys seats by the fire."

I watch my mom hurry up the path, then I turn my

attention back to the rectory. Niall plans on having wood floors installed, but that will come after the restorations are mostly complete. A part of me thinks I'll miss the old cavernous ruins. Every time I'm in there, I think of Logan. I see him everywhere. I hear him, his voice in my ear. And even though our kiss wasn't an actual kiss, I still feel the static electricity of his lips brushing mine. Absently, with my fingertips, I touch my lips.

"Laird!" a young excavator suddenly says, hurrying at an excited jog out of the rectory and across the small area of grass toward Niall. "Sir!"

I notice the excavator holds something in his hands. He's cradling it away from his body, but careful just the same. The excavator is tall and lanky, with a shock of auburn hair and wide blue eyes, with skin as pale as note-book paper. He wears a badge that says *Rob* on it.

"Aye?" Niall asks as the boy stops before us.

"We found this, Laird," Rob says. He holds his trea-sure, wrapped in a heavy cloth of some sort, out to Niall.

Niall looks at it. "What is it?"

"Och, if you dunna mind, sir," Rob says, pushing the object closer. "Go ahead and take it?" Niall does, and Rob visibly sighs in relief. Rob shoves his gloved hands in his coat pockets. Niall pulls the cloth off, revealing something small, aged. "'Tis a flute," Rob says, "entwined with —"

"Rowan," I say, almost a whisper. I can't take my eyes off of it. Could it be Logan's?

"Aye," Rob says. "Twisted rowan." He shudders. "'Tis cursed."

"Och, boy," Niall says. He quickly unwinds the rowan from the flute and tosses the bark to the ground, stomping it with his heel. "There's no such thing —"

A wave of . . . *something* passes over the courtyard. Almost like another sonic boom. It reminds me of the sound the ring and spell book made when they burst out of sight. The trees visibly shake, and I teeter where I stand. I feel the sensation pass through me. Everyone stops what they're doing. They're all looking around, their expressions masks of disbelief.

I glance at Niall. "What was *that*?" I ask.

"I dunno," Niall answers. We both look at Rob. He is, if possible, even whiter than before.

He takes off running to the rectory.

Niall seems unbothered by the event. He barely even acknowledges it happened.

It did, though. What exactly it was, I haven't a clue. But I can't shake the feeling that it was something important. Resonant.

Niall stares down at the flute. With his thumb, he wipes an area clean. He looks at me. "Initials, Ivy," he says, and he holds it down low enough for me to see.

I gasp. *LM* is etched into the instrument.

"'Tis quite old," Niall says, turning the flute over in his hands and inspecting it. "I canna imagine what it was buried beneath the rectory for. Would you like to have it?" he asks.

Excitement floods me. I nod. "Yes." Niall hands it to me. I'm sure he has no idea that the initials mean Logan Munro, but I know. My heart is racing.

With the wind biting into my face, I stare down at the instrument through tear-filled eyes. I have no doubt the relic belonged to Logan. And now it all makes sense: His cousin, Patrick — driven mad by that ruby ring — must have murdered Logan by wrapping a personal possession of Logan's in rowan. Cursing it.

I try to hold back my tears, telling Niall that I have a sudden headache. He looks a bit concerned but waves me off and goes to speak to the excavators about something.

I make it back to my room, short of breath and clutching Logan's prized flute. I set it down on the trunk at the foot of my bed, unsure what exactly to do with it. I pace the length of my room, my thoughts swirling. The flute, the rowan, that strange sound. Logan . . . I can't help but feel that something has shifted. But what?

I know there's only one way I can truly feel settled. I wait until the late afternoon, when the excavators are finished for the day. Then I grab my violin and bow, tuck the flute in my pocket, and steal out of the castle. I make my way back to the rectory. The sun is setting, striping the gray clouds purple. The skies are so dramatic here, and so vast. It almost doesn't seem real, like I'm in some kind of enchanted fairyland where nothing is as it appears.

The rectory is deserted now — the excavators having left for the night and Niall back in the castle with Mom, both of them convinced I'm up in my room with a headache.

I know Niall is right — that the construction site isn't quite safe. But as I pick my way carefully into the rectory, it doesn't even feel that different. The ground is patchy and shaky but I know now that no invisible hands will be shoving me. Slowly, I make my way over to the stone seat by the window.

Setting Logan's flute on the stone beside me, I pick up my violin, and drag my bow over the strings. The melody I play is the one I composed when I first arrived here. Haunting. Serene. It reminds me of Logan. It's the piece I'll be playing at the Strings festival. I play for several moments, my eyes closed.

Suddenly, a sensation rushes through me, and I stop. For no good reason, my heartbeat quickens. It slams into my chest and against my ribs with such force, so out of control, that I think something's wrong. I set the violin and bow down, and press my hand against my heart. It's beating fast and hard.

"Ivy."

My brain can't get the messages to my body quick enough. I dare not believe what I hear, even as my back stiffens and I slowly turn to the sound of my name.

My eyes fall on the figure standing in the still-crumbled opening that was once the rectory's doorway. I stare, trembling, disbelieving.

I mouth his name. No words escape. They're trapped.

The figure moves toward me.

"There's no way I'll believe you canna speak, lass," the figure says teasingly, moving closer to me. His boots scrape against the packed dirt as his swaggering stride closes the distance between us. A grin spreads across his painfully handsome face. "No way."

"Logan?" I whisper, drinking him in. Suddenly, I'm standing, but my legs are locked into place. Inside, I'm shaking. "Is it you?"

Chapter 22

GRATEFUL

$\mathscr{I}$ can't stop looking at him. Are my eyes playing tricks on me? I blink several times and even shake my head. When I focus, the Logan-like figure is standing less than a foot away.

His thumb grazes my cheek. . . .

My eyes widen; I can feel his touch, his skin against mine. The warmth of his thumb against my skin.

We can touch.

Logan lowers his head toward me, smiling.

"I have dreamed of this," he whispers, then settles his lips against my mouth.

And he kisses me.

His full lips move over mine, and my heart soars with joy, disbelief. My knees grow weak, and Logan must sense it because he holds me tightly against him. My arms fly around his neck in a fierce embrace.

I'm afraid to let go.

"I can't believe you're here," I whisper against his neck. I'm trembling. I can smell him. Smell his clean skin. Feel the warmth of his live body seep through his clothes — which are the same clothes he's worn since I first met him. Dark, hand-sewn pants, boots, and the white shirt. His dark hair is loose and wavy against his collar, and I swear, he's the most handsome thing I've ever seen.

"You're here, alive." I pull back and look up into his familiar silver eyes. "How?" I ask. "How is it even possible?"

Logan's gaze never leaves mine, but his hands move to cup my face.

"I'm not sure," he answers, still studying my features as if he's never seen them before. It's as if he's discovered something brand-new. He laughs softly. "All I know is, I suddenly popped up in the village, and I was real. Alive again. And I knew I had to find you." He kisses me. "I dunna want tae let you go, Ivy Calhoun."

It must have had something to do with unearthing Logan's flute. The sonic boom that followed, the unease that had settled? I reach for the flute and hand it to Logan.

He grasps it with one hand, studies it. Runs his thumb over his initials. Then he looks at me and smiles.

And never have I felt so happy.

We stand in the ruined rectory, enveloped in each other's arms. Outside, the wintry wind howls, but I barely notice it as Logan Munro's heart beats strong against my ear and I melt against his warm embrace.

I can't explain it. Right now, I don't even care. Logan's back.

And he's mine.

"You look nervous."

Logan glances down at me, then gives me a mock frown. "I'm no' nervous, gell. I've met them all before." He cockily jerks his jaw upward and stands rigid, then grabs the enormous iron knocker and bangs it.

I can do little more than smile, link my arm through his, and wait for the Munros' door to open.

After we'd left the rectory that night, we had shocked old Ian and Jonas with Logan's return. Mom and Niall had taken Elizabeth to the village for fish-and-chips, so we had the place to ourselves for a bit. We had talked for hours and finally made sense of everything that had happened.

We realized that the moment Logan's flute was unearthed, there was a chance of reversing the curse. When Niall had pulled the twisted rowan off was when Logan had found himself back at Glenmorrag village, alive.

All of Logan's memories have returned as well. My theory wasn't totally correct, because Logan's uncle Patrick had not in fact killed him. When Logan discovered Patrick's spell book and the truth about his ring, Patrick had instead cursed Logan with the Veil of Death — which meant that he would remain suspended between life and death forever. Patrick had taken a personal article of Logan's — the flute — and wrapped it in cursed rowan, and hidden it beneath the old rectory. Just to ensure that the spell on Logan would never break.

When Logan's mother discovered what Patrick had done, she'd put two and two together and ripped the ruby ring off his finger, removing him from the sway of the dark spirit. But instead of healing, as Elizabeth had, Patrick went mad and threw himself off the seawall. Logan, in spirit form, saw his mother steal into the castle and hide the ruby ring and spell book. Both remained hidden until Elizabeth discovered them the night of the storm.

The ring was a black mark upon the Munro family. It had originated from a different clan, one who had feuded with the Munros back in the early Middle Ages. The ring was so powerful that whoever wore it could cast all kinds of spells — apparitions, pain, sickness . . . even death. In particular, the ring was dead set against newcomers, people it viewed as interlopers. That was why my mom and I had been its targets when Elizabeth wore it.

It wasn't until Emma and I destroyed the ring, and the spell book, that its power disappeared for good. And it wasn't until Niall removed the rowan from Logan's flute that his particular enchantment had broken. Logan was free.

And I am ever so glad. Now that Logan is alive again, at eighteen, he will live out his life. He'll go to school. I've already begun to teach him how to read. He'll play his flute, maybe learn a new instrument.

Logan stayed overnight in Ian's croft, but today, Jonas drove us over to the Munro keep after I got out of school. Logan wants to learn to drive, too. To learn everything. But we have time. So much time.

As we wait for the door to open, Logan, sensing my

stare, glances down at me. His mercury eyes soften, and one corner of his mouth lifts in a slight grin. I want to fling my arms around him. It's very difficult to keep from touching him at all times, now that I can.

The enormous door to the keep opens, and Ethan Munro stands in the archway. All six foot seven inches of him. Ethan stares at Logan, inspecting him from head to toe. Then he gives a nod.

"Och, boy," he says, amazement tingeing his heavy accent. He pulls Logan into a fierce hug, and Logan hugs him back. Then Ethan Munro looks at me and grins.

"You're a strong lass, Ivy," he says, then drops a kiss to my cheek. He turns back to Logan, who still stands rigidly tall with his chin lifted, meeting his ancestor's gaze. Ethan puts his hand on Logan's shoulder. "Come inside, boy, and I'll show you to your room. You'll fit in just fine here, I vow it."

Logan squeezes my hand and follows Ethan inside. Ethan looks over his shoulder at me and, with eyes the exact same color as Logan's, winks.

"Ivy! Logan!" Amelia says, appearing at my side. She hugs us both. "Come inside before you freeze!"

I grin and step into the Munro keep. Logan's new home. Filled with Logan's ancestors from long ago.

This is the place that taught me that the impossible can be possible.

"Come on," Amelia says, pulling me along the corridor to the kitchen. "I've got a can of Cheez Whiz with your name on it, girl. And I want to talk to you about a new story idea I have."

I smile at her. Amelia is the most likable person I've ever met. Well, almost. She definitely ranks up with the top three anyway.

As I watch Logan Munro swagger up the spiral steps, still dressed in his nineteenth-century clothes, I know I've witnessed magic. And miracles.

And I'm so grateful for both.

I mean, I'm in a keep full of once-enchanted fourteenth-century warriors. My once-ghost boyfriend's new home.

Then, in the next instant, Logan rushes back down the stairs. He pulls me into a tight embrace, his mouth to my ear.

"*Mairidh mo ghaol gu siorraidh*, Ivy Calhoun," he whispers.

I smile at him. "I'll love you forever, too."

With a grin, he races away.

Somewhere above, several deep laughs break out.

I smile. Grateful doesn't even begin to describe it.

Epilogue

The twinkling lights in the ancient kirk emit amber hues over the stone walls. The crowd gathered in the seating area below the stage are cast in shadows. Only in the first few rows are the faces visible.

I'm here. At the Strings of the Highlands festival. In Inverness. Wicked sweet.

Sir Malcolm Catesby, famed violinist, is in the audience somewhere. The thought makes me sweat a little.

But in the front row, Logan's stare is fastened directly onto mine, and I smile.

Nervous butterflies beat a crazy rhythm inside of my stomach. I can't believe I'm one of the violinists competing. It blows my mind completely. There are twelve of us and we stand in a single row across the stage.

Emma helped me pick out my dress last night. It's a simple black shift, with a pair of black strappy heels that aren't too daring or high. They're just right. She insisted that I wear my hair down, and I did. She says the black dress shows off my sassy pink streak. I hope she's right.

I glance into the audience again. Emma is sitting beside Logan, and she's holding hands with Serrus. Next comes my mom, now hugely pregnant and beaming. Then Niall and, yes, Gran Elizabeth — the last person I'd thought would be showing up to support me. She looks serene and proud. They'd met Logan, who I'd introduced as a cousin come to live with the Munros, and had instantly taken a liking to him. Jonas is here, too, and even Ian cleaned up for the event.

I can't see the second row, but I know it's made up entirely of the other Munros. Amelia, Ethan, his brothers and cousins. I shake my head. I still can't fully grasp everything that's transpired.

Headmistress Worley is seated off to the side, and I catch her gaze. She gives me a thumbs-up.

I'm number seven down the line of violinists, and the first six are phenomenal. My nerves are jumpy, but every time I look at Logan he smiles, and immediately, I feel calm again.

"And for your pleasure, next is our lovely American, Miss Ivy Calhoun, playing her own composition, 'Forevermore.'" The director nods to me, giving me my cue to begin.

The lights dim, all except the one centered on me. I let everything wash through me, over me, all that's happened since I first set foot at Glenmorrag. It races through my veins and winds its way to my fingertips like a live thing. My arm lifts, sets the bow, and slowly, I begin to play. Every emotion I feel, for my dad, my mom and Niall, my soon-to-be siblings, my new friends, and even old Elizabeth, pours into my melody.

Especially my feelings for Logan Munro. They have become my muse.

Everything inside of me is silent, save the music.

And I play. The melody starts out haunting. I change tempo, and add that something extra that makes the music mine. It's sometimes frowned upon, but I've learned to accept me for me.

And this is my music. My way. My bow flies over my

strings, faster, faster, and then slows. The music evokes the ghostly spirit of the Highlands.

When I finish, I'm out of breath. The applause is deafening. It's what brings me back to the stage, from the place I go to when I sink into my song. My gaze finds Logan's, and he's standing with the rest of them, clapping so hard and grinning so widely, my heart soars.

Then he mouths the words *I love you*.

I smile, and then I laugh. *I love you, too,* I mouth in return.

I realize it doesn't matter if I win the contest or not.

This is my life. My destiny.

Unbelievable stuff. Stuff you find only in fairy tales.

Except this time, it happened for *real*. Logan's for real.

And he's all mine.

Forevermore.

Acknowledgments

To the following, I owe way more than mere gratitude and thanks. I owe you a piece of my heart for helping Ivy, Logan, and *Forevermore* leave the recesses of my imagination and become a reality.

My mom, Dale Nease, is my biggest fan, and her constant love and support will be with me until I'm old and gray. My daughter, Tyler, is always there to listen to my ideas and keep my voice young. My best friend and author sister, Kim Ungar, is there for daily chats, brainstorming, recipe swapping, encouragement, and all-around life. I don't know what I'd do without her.

My fantastic agent, Deidre Knight of the Knight Agency, is so much more than an agent to me. She believed in *Forevermore* and me, and for that I'm eternally grateful. My editors, Aimee Friedman and Becky Shapiro, helped me realize *Forevermore* in a whole new light. Their input/editing/ideas have been magic! Artist Tricia Cramblet and cover designer Yaffa Jaskoll brought Ivy and Logan to life on the book's cover. Such a beautiful and fantastic job!

Best friends and Wolfpack — you know who you are — keep me laughing, living life to the fullest, and are always encouraging. We will have the funniest memories long into our elder years! Long-time pal, world travel buddy, and sister author, Leah Marie Brown, and I have shared many crazy adventures, and they'll always inspire my life and writing.

And finally, Angus J. Maclennan is owner and proprietor of the fabulous Ivy Cottage in the Highlands of Scotland, and was also my landlord there for two and half weeks. Ivy Cottage's lands are complete with ancient standing stones and close to dozens of historical sites and castles, and were and are sheer inspiration for my writing. A true and proud Scotsman from the ancient Isle of Lewis, Angus, along with his sister, Ishbel Maclennan, helped me with the beautiful Gaelic language used in *Forevermore*. Ishbel also supplied the gorgeous Scottish Proverb that opens the story. To actually hear the Gaelic language spoken is pure enchantment! Thanks again to Angus, his wife, Fiona, and their adorable Highland dancing daughter, Emma, and Shep, their naughty fence-jumping sheepdog! It was the most memorable and inspiring trip to Scotland I've ever experienced! Without all of you, the story simply wouldn't mean so much to me.

There's more than one way to be powerful....

ABBY SILVA HAS JUST LEARNED THAT SHE'S descended from accused witches who lived in 1600s Salem. When Abby visits Salem and falls for a handsome local boy, strange, otherworldly things begin to happen. Candles burst into flame, and an ancient spell book winds up in her possession. Could Abby possibly have powers of her own?

DON'T MISS *Spellbinding,* THE GRIPPING NOVEL BY MAYA GOLD!

this is teen

Want to find more books, authors, and readers to connect with?

Interact with friends and favorite authors, participate in weekly author Q&As, check out event listings, try the book finder, and more!

Join the new social experience at
www.facebook.com/thisisteen